SISTERS AT WAR

The Strong Family Saga
Book One

Ros Rendle

SAPERE
BOOKS

SISTERS AT WAR

Published by Sapere Books.

20 Windermere Drive, Leeds, England, LS17 7UZ,
United Kingdom

saperebooks.com

ISBN: 978-1-80055-083-4

To Scott, for his research help and support.

ACKNOWLEDGEMENTS

Thanks go to Scott Rendle for his research into battles of the First World War and for his company when we visited those places. He has also been very supportive of my writing and the long process of producing a book.

The Romantic Novelists' Association has a New Writers' Scheme which allows aspiring authors to receive a comprehensive report for a manuscript. Before I graduated from this scheme with the publication of my previous book, *Sense and French Ability*, I received such a critique for *Sisters at War*. It was extremely helpful, and I should like to thank the RNA for this scheme. I have made many friends with generosity of spirit in the RNA, but particular thanks go to Julie for her support and advice.

All the people at Sapere Books have been truly amazing in the skill and patience they have demonstrated. Together we have produced this book which is the first in the Strong Family Historical Saga series. Thank you to each of the team.

Thanks also go to my followers and supporters on Twitter and Facebook, many of whom I have since met in person at conferences and meetings.

CHAPTER 1

September 1913

Rose Strong's shoulders sagged as she sank onto the edge of the bed, the linen underskirt destined for the trunk crumpled in her hands. This eve of her first journey away from her family at only just eighteen years of age, was a huge thing. Her papa's words circled. "There are no secrets to success," he said often enough. "Preparation, learning and hard work." But Rose had another secret. It made leaving her home and this place even harder.

She heard her sisters' voices drifting up the stairs. Should she share her secret desires with them before her departure? Lady Margaret Hall at the University of Oxford was such a long way and although she had dreamed of it forever, now the time was here, she suddenly felt a pang for the life she was going to leave behind.

Their voices and laughter came nearer. Despite all their faults, and probably hers too, she loved her sisters dearly. The door crashed open and Delphi came tumbling into the bedroom. Her face was flushed, and she put up a hand to straighten her thick hair in a familiar gesture, although it wasn't needed. "What on earth are you doing sitting there, Rose? Come along, you're only halfway packed. You're not taking your lilac shawl while you are gone, are you? I was hoping I might borrow it. It matches my new dress so well."

"I don't know why you're asking. You usually just take it anyway." Rose raised her eyes to her beautiful, wayward middle sister and wished she had half her good looks. No, she would not share her secret just now. Nobody but a sister knew your vulnerability, and Delphi would aim for that with no mercy. Much as Rose loved her and tried to understand her, she knew of Delphi's need to be first in everything.

Izzy had followed her older sibling into the room. "May I help you, Rose?"

"Yes, dearest, that would be lovely." Rose stood again and folded the petticoat before handing it to her youngest sister to place in the trunk.

"I shall miss you so much," Izzy said.

"And I you, but you are twelve now and growing into a fine young lady. It won't be long before you are having an adventure such as I."

"I'm never going away. I shall stay here and look after Mama and Papa and Hector too, if he's still here. I suppose he'll go into the army, though. I shall play the piano for them each evening." Izzy smiled.

"Don't be such a silly noddle, Iris," Delphi said, using her little sister's given name.

"And don't you be mean to me, *Delphinium*."

"Don't call me that." Delphi slammed her hand down on the surface of the dressing table. "Ridiculous name."

"Girls, please. Did you come to help me or what?" Rose said, slipping into her habitual role of keeping the peace.

"Everyone's going away except for me," Delphi moaned.

"Not everyone, Delphi dear, and you could go next year when you are old enough, if you continue to study as Papa says you may."

"Huh! I have no desire to be a brainbox, as well you know. How dull. No, I shall find a very suitable husband and he will keep me in the manner I desire."

Rose gave her a look, but it only hit Delphi between the shoulder blades as she turned back to the mirror and peered at the tendrils of dark chestnut hair artfully framing her high cheek-boned face. "I hear Michael Redfern is going away to college, too." Her voice was casual, but Rose saw Delphi glancing at her in the mirror's reflection. She turned away with haste.

"Really? Is he not taking over from his father at the department store?"

"I thought *you* would know, Rose," Delphi said.

Rose swallowed the lump in her throat, pushed her glasses back up her nose and touched her forehead where her frounce of hair, so difficult to tame, was bothering her. Had Delphi guessed her secret after all? "Me?" she said.

"I thought all you clever college types knew everything," Delphi said waspishly. "Papa seems to think you do."

"Well, that's because she *is* clever." Izzy leapt to Rose's defence. "Getting a place at Oxford is only for clever people."

Delphi chose to ignore this comment. "I'm going to see if lunch is nearly ready." She tossed her head and flounced out of the room.

"Why is Delphi always so … so difficult?" Izzy said. "Oh Rose, I shall miss you so." She crossed the room and flung her arms around Rose.

Rose looked up to the ornate plaster ceiling and blinked rapidly. "Come along, sweet, we'll finish off the last bits later." A gong sounded downstairs. "Delphi's right. Lunch must be about ready."

They walked along the landing and held hands as they descended the wide stairway. The smells of mutton and herbs wafted through the large hallway as they approached the dining room.

Delphi, their fourteen-year-old brother Hector, and their mother were there before them. Mr Strong entered the well-proportioned dining room and they all sat at the oval mahogany table.

"Well, Rose, all ready?"

"Nearly, Papa."

It was normal for this family, if unusual among their peers, to discuss major events around the dinner table. While Mr Strong was strict, he believed his girls, as well as his son, should have every educational opportunity open to them. They were fortunate. Their mother had often said, "You need to be able to converse with a future husband in an educated and informed way. Also, if, God forbid, one of you ends up as an independent woman, you will have something to fall back on, too. That's why he encourages you to be interested in current affairs. Be grateful, girls. You are born into a modern, caring and proper family."

"There is still unrest by these blasted suffragette women." Mr Strong shook a linen napkin and covered his lap. "Even in the Low Countries. Good grief, what more do they want here? They can even attend ladies' colleges to further their opportunities now, as you are doing, Rose. Thank goodness you are sensible."

The girls had long since learned that it was unwise to argue against their father's remarks. They were pleased to be included but had learned to play the game of saying little if they disagreed. On this occasion Rose could not resist, however, since it was a subject close to her own heart.

"Women can study and pass exams, but they cannot yet receive a degree," she offered. "That seems a little unfair."

Mr Strong regarded her before saying, "Ladies need not be so … unfeminine. It's ugly."

They finished the roast cod and asparagus sauce and waited for Dora, the cook, to waddle in with the mutton hotpot.

"Austria-Hungary are not satisfied," Mr Strong added. "It's all a bit of a ferment and many alliances are being struck, what with Germany backing Austria-Hungary, and our Great British Empire must decide whether it is for Russia or not."

"Why aren't we joining with Germany?" Hector asked.

Mr Strong cleared his throat. "Germany is getting too big for its boots. It's trying to dominate Europe, increasing its navy as well as its army. We can see Germany eyeing up some of our colonial territories. Can't be having that, now, can we?"

"All this talk of aggression," Mrs Strong ventured, "is tiresome at the table. Isn't there something more pleasant we can talk about? I was reading a report of the Horticultural Society yesterday afternoon. They had their first annual flower show at the Chelsea Hospital a couple of months ago. Do you think we might go to London next year for it? I should so love to do that, my dear."

"Oh, I should love to visit London," Delphi said and when Rose glanced across, her sister's eyes were shining, and her skin flushed.

"We shall certainly consider it," Mr Strong said.

Rose reverted to musing about her journey tomorrow as conversation meandered around the table. She was immensely grateful that Papa would be accompanying her on her first journey to Oxford. It was such a long way and quite nerve-racking.

How different would everything be when she returned at Christmas? Would she ever see Michael Redfern again, or would he meet someone else at the college to which he was going?

CHAPTER 2

"I cannot believe I am going to leave you," Rose said to her sisters the next morning as her luggage was taken out to the small carriage. She hugged them both and kissed her mother, trying to ignore the tears that threatened to fall from her mother's eyes. Rose's own were not far away, and her voice was in danger of cracking. Hector had to remain in the schoolroom, so she'd made her farewell to her younger brother already.

Rose took the seat next to her father, before Mr Yates flicked the reins and they lurched off. Since the route to Oxford was unfamiliar, Rose's father would travel with her, not only from home into town, but in the larger road coach to Manchester, and then the rest of the way by train.

"This journey to Lady Margaret Hall is exciting, is it not, Rose?"

"Yes, Papa." Rose's mind was on her family. It was the first time they had been apart, and her thoughts tumbled in a kaleidoscope of haphazard images from the past weeks. Delphi, nearly seventeen, already stunning in her beauty despite the frown creasing her pale complexion when Dora had called her Miss Delphinium. "Please do not use that name," she had wailed yet again. "You know I hate it." Rose softened inside at the memory.

"Delphinium's a beautiful name," the old retainer had said. "It means fun and strong-hearted, and Rose is just like her name too. Peace and happiness, grace, and sweetness. I'm not sure about the 'secret love' bit, though."

Then little Izzy invaded Rose's thoughts. Always interested in world affairs, even at her tender age. Izzy was still a child and frequently the butt of Delphi's jibes. Rose was always the pacifier between them.

The carriage pulled into the stable yard.

"Oh, Michael Redfern is approaching us. Is he travelling too?" Mr Strong peered out of the window.

Rose's head jerked around and her heart started pumping faster as she saw him.

It transpired that Michael was to travel in the same coach from their small town to Manchester. Rose was all of a jitter at the news.

"I hadn't realised that you were travelling today," she managed to say.

"I am to go by train from the city, too," Michael told them. "But my route is more direct to Peterborough and I don't need to change."

"We must journey to Crewe and thereafter on to Oxford," Mr Strong said. "What with carriage, coach and train it's quite a haul. Wait here, Rose. Michael, you will watch over her for a moment, won't you? I'm going to ascertain that all is well and that we are to leave on time. We don't want to miss our connections in Manchester."

"Oh, but…" Rose stood awkwardly in the company of her secret love and was bewildered by the strength of her longing. She would delight in being like Delphi and at ease with chatting and flirting but was uncertain what to say now she and Michael were alone. She glanced up at him, and noticing the scar peering from under his blond hair, she was transported back to the day they were first alone together.

She and her sisters had been walking home through the lane when the peace was shattered by a lot of clattering and shouting.

Izzy had grabbed Rose's arm and whispered, "I don't like it, Rose. What should we do? It may not be safe to venture further."

There had been an ear-splitting bellow and Hector had come bounding towards them.

Seeing his sisters, he had called out, "That stupid fellow has walloped Michael good and proper. We were play-acting, but he's done it now."

"What do you mean?" Izzy had wailed.

Delphi had run ahead, holding onto her hat with one hand.

The sisters had followed Hector through the trees to where Michael stood with his head bowed. The deep gash on his forehead dripped unheeded, forming a violent splash on his white shirt. A long log of wood lay at his feet, and three other lads looked aghast but clueless.

Delphi had berated them. "You're fighting with sticks! What on earth for? Hector, you should know better."

Rose had seen the way Michael had looked at Delphi, admiring her beautiful face with its prominent high cheekbones, and she had felt a pang of envy. But she had taken control and sent Hector to notify Michael's mother of the injury while Delphi and Izzy rushed ahead to the house to warn their mother to prepare some bandages.

Left alone with Michael, a flutter had passed through Rose. With her heart thumping, she had said, "We'll take the track through the trees to our house. It's closest and Mama will patch you up."

Boldly, since they were alone, she took his elbow to guide him over the rough ground. She glanced sideways and up at his face. She passed him her handkerchief and after holding it to the wound, he stumbled against her.

"Sorry, I can't see too well," he apologised. "The blood's running into my eyes."

He was quite a bit taller than she, so they staggered together along the trodden path until they came to the boundary of the family's property.

Rose's mother had met them on the path outside the house and Rose had distanced herself from Michael's lean frame.

Now, Rose was deeply aware of Michael as they stood together, smothered in a blanket of awkwardness, as they waited side by side for the return of her father. Rose blurted the first thing she could think of beyond their shared history.

"Papa has been tempted to buy a motor car. He had his eye on a lovely T-model Ford — I heard him discussing it with Mama. The price has dropped dramatically in the last four or five years, but they said the cost of my college course has delayed his decision for the time being."

She flushed, thinking she was spouting nonsense in her confusion. Why was she talking of motor cars when she had Michael to herself for a few moments? Why couldn't she talk easily and coquettishly like Delphi?

"That would be very exciting." Michael sounded stilted too.

She glanced up at him and he looked away quickly, brushing the sleeve of his jacket as if to remove some dust.

As Mr Strong returned, the road coach arrived. "Let me help you up, flower," the carriage starter said as he helped Rose to board the vehicle and then turned to load her cases and hatbox.

Rose surreptitiously glanced as often at Michael, sitting opposite, as the landscape. She let her imagination run away with her. She imagined their next meeting when he might take her arm and help her to a seat while he bowed his knee and presented her with flowers. Or maybe he would swirl her around in a waltz. A smile played at the corners of her mouth as she fantasised. Then she caught Michael glancing at her and felt a warm flush spread up her body. Maybe he was watching her as she was him.

"Tell me of the course you are to study, Michael," Mr Strong said.

Michael became animated. "St Peter's College for teacher training in Peterborough, sir, was built by the Diocese and opened in 1859, so they have a long history and a good reputation for religion and thoroughness. I shall be experiencing a classroom during the next term. It seems so soon, but the tutors feel we should have a taste of this in case some do not find teaching to their liking after all."

"I wish you good fortune then, young man," replied Mr Strong. "I think you'll do well, and our youngsters will be in safe hands."

They arrived at Manchester's London Road station and Rose and her father made their farewells to Michael Redfern.

Rose's thoughts wandered once again. *I wonder when we shall meet him again. I fear we shall both be changed so much that I will not know him.*

CHAPTER 3

After a frenetic term of learning, laughter and fun, Rose arrived back at her parents' home for the Christmas vacation.

After a day of recovery, she had one last errand to complete before the festivities.

"Can I come?" Izzy asked, leaning over the banister rail to talk to Rose below.

"Not this time, sweetheart. Some things must remain a secret until Christmas." She winked up at her youngest sister.

Rose caught the motor omnibus from the stop at the end of the road into the centre of the small town. She walked confidently along the pavement towards Redfern's Department Store. The skirt of her long wool coat swung with her jaunty step and the blue of her dress beneath matched the feathers in her hat. She caught glimpses of herself in shop windows and her reflection smiled back at her.

She had bought most of her Christmas gifts while away. Though small, she eked them out of her allowance, most of which had been spent on books and writing equipment. All she had left was a last present for Izzy.

I wonder if I will see Michael. She knew this was the nub of her eagerness. *The colleges all finish around the same time, so he should be home for Christmas.* Her heart beat faster than normal in anticipation.

As soon as Rose entered the store, Michael's mother spotted her.

"Why, Rose, how delightful. You must be home for Christmas."

"Yes, Mrs Redfern. The term finished on 17th December, and I arrived home yesterday. How are the girls?"

Mrs Redfern smiled at the mention of her daughters, Michael's two sisters. "Pretoria is always busy, and Tamsin is growing fast. Michael just came home too," she said. "I am sure he would like to see you."

Warmth spread up Rose's neck and she hoped she was too well muffled for Mrs Redfern to notice. She swallowed. "That would be lovely," she said. "I've just come to choose a gift for Izzy first."

"What did you have in mind? I imagine something pretty and delicate."

"Yes, exactly that," Rose agreed.

They settled on a light scarf, the peach shades of which suited Izzy's delicate colouring.

"Shall the girl charge it to Mr Strong's account as usual?"

"No, thank you. It's a gift directly from me, and I would like to use some of my allowance —"

A voice nearby made her start.

"Hello, Rose," came Mr Redfern's Northern accent. "Home from that smart ladies' college, are you?"

She turned to see Mr Redfern as he arrived behind her. He was a sizeable man with rosy cheeks and whiskers that marched across his face in abundance. His waistcoat was tight across his girth, but his height helped him to carry his weight. He was so different to his fulsome, careful wife. He always had a jovial smile and a twinkle in his hazel eyes. Rose smiled with genuine affection. She imagined he had small paper bags full of mint humbugs or sugared almonds in his pockets at all times.

"Yes, I came in to buy this for my sister," she responded, showing him the scarf.

"Michael would love to see you, I am certain. You will have much to talk about, now. Have you time to take a coffee? We have a new area in the shop. We call it Summer Court. Got to give people a feeling of well-being even though it's winter, eh?" He chuckled. "I believe Michael is there now. Come with me and I'll show you."

Rose settled her bill and took her purchase from the young woman behind the counter.

As she followed the speedy step of Mr Redfern, she passed artistic displays of gloves and scarves, prettily arranged. "What do you think of those, eh?" He didn't wait for a response. Further on, creams and potions to hydrate the skin lay artfully at different levels among yards of snowy silk and net. Rose was aware briefly of a delicate and refined scent as she hurried behind Mr Redfern. She glanced at a rainbow of hats displayed on little vertical rods that showed them off to perfection. Some were small and pert with dainty net, while others had feathers and bows and wide brims.

Rose took in all that she saw, but it didn't distract her from her nervous anticipation.

"All the latest things here, don't you know." Mr Redfern waved his hand vaguely at the display.

Scurrying behind him, further on still, sets of china plates and cups with silver spoons lay on a table as if for afternoon tea. A myriad of items could be purchased here, and all looked tempting. Rose knew of areas for ladies' fashions and clothing for gentleman with the attendant accessories. While the store had a long way to go to match those in London or even the centre of Manchester, it had grown beyond recognition from its early days.

They entered through an archway decorated on either side with tall, waxy aspidistra and found small tables with pristinely white cloths. Each place setting anticipated afternoon tea. Mr Redfern gallantly pulled out a chair for Rose to be seated.

"You treat me like a princess," she said as she peered up at him, pushing her glasses back up her nose. "The store looks lovely."

He beckoned for service and instantly, it seemed to Rose, someone appeared to wait upon her. She glanced all around, looking for Michael, her heart pumping violently. She became quite breathless.

"Is my son here today?" Mr Redfern demanded of the waiter.

"I'm sure he is, sir. Shall I send the boy to find him?"

"Yes, please do."

Michael arrived. He still had the same tall stature and the eyes she remembered so well. Those were the eyes that had first caught Rose's attention. Wide, blue, bright summer's day eyes that sparkled with vitality; electric blue vivid irises rimmed with cobalt. Rose was mesmerised by them. She could hardly pull her own away. She remembered how Michael's gaze had turned to Delphi as she sat across the room on the day he had been injured. Her sister had been cross because there was no seat more central in the small gathering when she'd returned to the room, having organised refreshment as Mother requested. As he'd looked across at her, Michael's gaze had become scrutinising, analytical, and Rose remembered nibbling her bottom lip with a sigh and a shrinking in her chest. She'd watched him stare at Delphi, and his lips had parted as he drew breath. There had been no doubt about his thoughts as far as Rose could see. Delphi, realising his gaze was upon her, had straightened her back and turned on her brightest smile.

Now, Rose could still see the scar on his temple. His blond hair tended to tumble forwards, and he brushed it back in a way that was familiar to her. However, in the few intervening months his shoulders had broadened and he had grown a presence that was not there before.

"You look every inch a gentleman," she heard herself say.

A smile spread across his face. "Rose, this is a surprise, how good to see you. May I?" He indicated the seat opposite her, and she nodded. As he pulled out the chair, another cup and saucer appeared for him. This gave him the moments he needed to gather his breath and his composure.

"It's lovely to be here," she said.

It wasn't long before things eased a little and a flurry of questions, answers and anecdotes occurred during the next three quarters of an hour. The time flew on. Michael described his college quarters and the people.

"There is an ancient well in the grounds where the chaps gather to smoke. I tried but I shan't be taking to it. The taste was foul and made me choke," he confessed with a grin. "The tennis courts will be good fun in the spring. They are right behind the college."

He went on to tell her about his encounters with tutors, his colleagues and the city of Peterborough itself with its fine cathedral right in the centre.

"You go through an archway and as soon as you do, it is so peaceful and quiet in the precincts. It's hard to remember that the noise of the streets is a few yards away. I'd love you to visit sometime. You would appreciate the history. Queen Katharine of Aragon is buried there."

Rose described some of the friends she had made, the lectures she had attended and the beautiful grounds of her college on the banks of the River Cherwell.

Michael spoke again. "I had my first experience of teaching a real class near the end of the term. It was only for two weeks."

"That must have been so exciting."

"I was in a village school just outside Peterborough, called Orton Waterville. For the first couple of days there were hardly any pupils arriving because they were out working the land on a harvest of sugar beet. There is a big processing plant just outside the city. Apparently, it's acceptable to be absent under those terms. Anyway, when the pupils returned, I told them they needed to 'pull up their socks' and work hard to make up for their absence. Well, it's just a figure of speech, isn't it? They bent over and started literally pulling up their socks. Talk about awkward! So stupid of me. I shan't make that mistake again."

Rose laughed at his story and he relaxed.

As she began to gather her things prior to leaving, Rose noticed another young man approaching them. His wide mouth formed a cheerful smile. While his nose was a little large for his face and his hair unfashionably curly, there was a warmth about this friend, an optimism defying any criticism of the physical problems which caused his uneven gait and resulted in the need for a walking stick.

There were introductions. Michael explained that Thom's father worked in the store as a senior buyer. "They have recently moved here from Cardiff in Wales, so he knows few people."

"Rose, how lovely to meet you. Michael, your father said you were in here."

Michael asked, "Shall we sit and have more tea? Do you have the time, Rose?"

"Yes, by all means."

"I hear you have started a course at Oxford, Rose? Very impressive," Thom said. "Are you home for Christmas? You must be pleased to see your family. Are you enjoying it?"

His questions were non-stop as he sat and laid his stick on the floor next to the table. "I'm sorry," he grinned. "I'm firing questions and not pausing for the replies."

Rose smiled back at him. "It's very good, and yes, it's good to see the family, thank you." She glanced at Michael. "Someone's been talking about me."

An endearing flush spread around his neck and Michael looked down at his lap, brushing off some imaginary piece of fluff from his knees.

They talked about Rose's term. "I'm studying Greek and Latin, all the usual things, but there's an emphasis on English literature and history, too. I know, as a woman, I'm not allowed to receive a degree, but I am able to study and pass exams. I'm so fortunate that Papa says I may be there."

They moved onto respective plans for the forthcoming season of social activities, and Michael asked Thom if he came wanting anything in particular.

"I was passing, see, and thought to find out if you were going to the Blackshaw's Christmas party. I shan't go if you're not, as I shall know few others there."

"I think we are going," Rose offered.

"I'll be there too," Michael added.

"Well, that's spiffing then, isn't it?" Thom replied in his slight Welsh lilt. "I shall really look forward to it now." He smiled at Rose.

CHAPTER 4

Christmas 1913 had the usual traditions. It was a time of great importance to Rose, who much appreciated the closeness of family. The girls and Hector had already spent several afternoons making chains from interlinked loops of paper and now they were draped across the ceiling in bright swathes of colour. The tree stood in the corner of the drawing room, and all the decorations the siblings had gathered throughout their childhood hung from the branches.

Church came first with all the family walking under the porch of the lychgate and up the path in threes. Behind Papa, Mama and Hector, Delphi, Rose and Izzy also greeted friends. The family attended most weeks, but Christmas was always an extra special occasion for meeting and exchanging news.

"I imagine the Redferns will be here," Delphi said as she wound tendrils of dark hair around her fingers and smoothed her skirt. "I'm pleased with my new hat. Does this colour suit me, Rose?"

"You well know that it does, dearest." Rose was used to her sister's preening and on occasion it riled her, but today was Christmas Day and she was prepared to be more generous of spirit. She, too, hoped that they would see Michael and his family.

As they neared the people milling about outside the church, a young man broke away from the crowd. Michael approached and Delphi patted her hair again and pulled her cuffs straight as she stepped forwards. "Well, if it isn't Michael Redfern. What a surprise," she fibbed with flirting eyes. "Why,

Michael," she continued, looking up at him through her long, dark lashes, "is that for me?"

He looked abashed and glanced at the small parcel he carried.

Rose guessed, from the finger that ran around his collar and the pursing of his lips, that her sister's teasing was making him uncomfortable.

"I need a word with Rose," he said, deftly stepping past the younger sister.

Delphi sighed and rolled her eyes.

"Michael?" Rose put out her hand to receive the small flat package. "What is this?"

"I owe you this. It's not as fine as the one you lent me," he said as she pulled off the dainty wrapping, "but I hope you like it well enough, and it will replace the one I managed to ruin when we boys had that silly argument at the end of the summer."

"Why, thank you, Michael. It has a little pink rose on it, too. Look, Delphi, how pretty it is," she said, showing her sister the new handkerchief. "It wasn't necessary for you to replace mine."

With that, he inclined his head and wished them a merry Christmas before he turned with haste. Rose secreted the handkerchief in her pocket but decided to place it reverently in her little box on the dressing table. She would preserve it there for all time and certainly never use it for its intended purpose.

Eating vast quantities, present-giving and receiving, and singing around the fire in the evening were all festive customs with which Rose had grown up, and they were dear to her. Dora excelled herself and the table was groaning with the weight of the food, as were the family by the time they had consumed the cod poached in parsley sauce, followed by an enormous turkey with mountains of vegetables grown by the farmer down the lane, and crispy roasted potatoes cooked in succulent goose fat. The pudding was carried in with great ceremony, and Mr Strong set it alight with a measure of brandy after it was placed before him by Dora. Then she removed it to the sideboard to be served with lashings of custard.

Rose was pleased with the reactions from her brother and two sisters to the gifts she had bought. Both parents were proud of the photograph she'd had commissioned of herself outside the college building, and joy seeped from Rose's heart as they placed it on the lid of the grand piano. Rose glanced at Delphi. A tiny frown scuttled across her sister's face.

They were so full of food the parlour games had to wait for an hour, but The Sculptor, always a favourite, made all the women cry with laughter as limbs were bent and placed by the one who was chosen for the part. Hector and Mr Strong played the game with gusto, and Hector managed to hold his pose the longest. He was rewarded with cheers and more laughter, at which he stood with his chest thrust out and feet apart, a satisfied smile quirking his mouth.

Mrs Strong's tears threatened to fall as her three girls sang 'In the Bleak Midwinter' with a harmony they had worked on together for several days. Izzy played the piano beautifully as always.

Later that evening, the three girls descended into the hall. "I am so excited about this party," Delphi said. They were dressed in their finery with complementary beads around their necks and feathers in their hair. "I would have loved to wear harem pants," she said.

"There is absolutely no way that Mama would allow that." Rose laughed at the idea. "That is typical of you, Delphi. You look lovely, so don't worry. That shade of peacock blue is daring enough for one of your age."

"What do you mean 'one of my age'?"

Rose sighed. "Nothing, dearest. You look stunning." *Everything's always on your own terms,* Rose thought. *Always distracted by what gives you the most limelight.*

Rose, pretty in her apple blossom pink voile which had an underskirt of a deeper shade, was content with how she looked. The embroidered panel at the front was decorated with bows, and she had lace across her décolletage as the main fabric of the neckline was cut in a fashionable V shape.

"No shocking the vicar," Mrs Strong smiled and gave a nod. "You all look lovely, girls."

Izzy was allowed the same style, but her dress was cinnamon gauze over satin. The waistband was embroidered with bugle beads, buttons and dainty rosettes.

As they arrived in the hall, Rose saw her Mama and Papa. "You are the most handsome parents in the street."

Mrs Strong wore black silk, tulle, and navy lace with blue sequins and bugle beads. Between her husband and her son in their evening attire, they were a matched trio.

The Blackshaw's Christmas party was a formal affair with a seated dinner followed by the ladies withdrawing so the gentlemen could enjoy their port and cigars. The younger generation had a room with a gramophone.

"Oh, how exciting." Delphi clapped her hands when she saw it. "Michael, go and wind it up. What music do we have? Let's dance."

Thom stood next to Rose. "Have you any plans for next week before you return to Oxford?"

"This vacation is a brief but social whirl," Rose replied.

"Perhaps when you return next, we might consider setting up an outing to the Kinemacolor in Manchester?"

"I'm not very familiar with the city. Where is the picture house?"

"It's between Oxford Road and Whitworth Street West. It's that large building right on the corner."

In her peripheral vision, as she tried to make polite conversation, Rose was aware of Delphi trying to encourage Michael to dance. He laughed with her and they looked so happy together. Her skin prickled. The tightening grip of her thoughts squeezed her lungs and made her heart thump. Life was so unfair. Why did she have to wear these stupid glasses? Why couldn't she have Delphi's voluptuous figure and luxurious hair instead of being slight with a frizz at her forehead? She wanted Michael to look at her like that instead of her sister.

She turned her attention back to Thom. "I'm sorry, what did you say they're showing?"

"They're due to show *The Prisoner of Zenda* soon with Beatrice Beckley and James Hackett. It sounds really good."

He does have very nice eyes, and he's a gentle fellow, Rose thought as she listened. "I've never been. Perhaps when I return, as you say. It sounds like fun."

As the music finished and the dancers subsided onto chairs and settees, Rose extricated herself from Thom's company and sat next to her middle sister.

"Delphi, it's not seemly to throw yourself at anyone the way you were casting yourself at Michael."

"You might be brainy and skilful with your paints and brushes, but you're not so clever about good looks and fashion," Delphi sniped back. "Really, Rose, you're turning into one of those awful 'Blue Stocking' women," she said.

"I'm not. Anyway, they go to Cambridge and I'm at Oxford. 'Sweet city with her dreaming spires,'" she quoted from Matthew Arnold's poem.

"Tch! It's not the Victorian age anymore. I don't need you to chaperone me." Delphi sighed as she turned away.

There was a crash and both girls looked over. Hector's raised voice rasped across the air.

"I was named for a hero. At our last Boy Scouts' meeting we saluted the flag and stood to attention. Our promise is to serve God, the King and our country. I must be a good and loyal citizen. We sang that song, you know." He straightened his shoulders and raised his chin.

"*Scouts will be Scouts*
Scouts can be heroes too
By striving to aid
A man or a maid
And seeing the Scout law through.
I am a person of courage, like I promise each week. I'm named for a hero, I tell you."

Rose hastened to his side, taking his shoulders and turning him away from his opponent. "Yes, you are, but you're a fourteen-year-old boy too, and it's Christmas. This generation is obsessed with heroism, and this is neither the time nor the place. Hush now."

"He said it was alright for the Germans to build more Dreadnoughts," Hector offered. "He said they were defending their rights. We *know* that the British offered to slow or even halt construction of those ships if Germany agreed to that limitation treaty thing. They said that in March, and it's Christmas now. What he said was traitorous." He cast a foul grimace back at the other boy.

"Hector! I said this is not the right time, and it's certainly not appropriate in this gathering. I repeat, it's Christmas. Go and get yourself a soothing drink of lemonade or maybe even one of the fruit sodas. You always had a taste for those. Forget this argument for now."

Taking a calming breath herself, Rose returned to the settee.

Rose and Delphi skirted around each other for the rest of the evening but as they prepared for bed that night, Rose put out the olive branch of peace to her middle sister. "Delphi, dearest, I know you were only enjoying yourself. I'm sorry if I sounded unintentionally harsh."

"Yes, well, I was only having fun."

"I know."

Delphi left to go to the bathroom and Izzy entered as Rose opened the lid of the little box and took a peek at the fabric with the embroidered rose that lay inside. "It's very pretty," Izzy said. "I think he likes you … a lot." As Delphi returned, Izzy added with artless enthusiasm, "I think Rose has a new beau."

Before Rose could respond, Delphi snapped at her, "No, she doesn't. Don't be a noddle head, Izzy."

"Girls! Please act like young ladies," admonished Mrs Strong gently but firmly as she came in to say goodnight. The antagonism between her middle and other two daughters was familiar to all of them.

Rose tried hard to see things from Delphi's point of view, but she knew at eighteen she didn't have the experience of their mother. Her mind drifted away to the conversation she had shared with her parent a few days ago.

"Mama, I understand that Izzy is still immature for her age, but I find Delphi so … so complicated," she had said. "She never seems satisfied. Either she says I get privileges because

I'm the eldest, or Izzy gets things easier because she's the youngest. Delphi has everything. She's beautiful and clever enough, but she always wants more than her fair share of attention."

"She does not have your quiet strength, my dearest. You are organised and conscientious. She is still a little insecure and finding her place. Nor does she have the sunny nature of Izzy to which others naturally respond. She has always tended to be rebellious." Her mother had sighed.

Rose came back to the present and looked at her sister. She was determined to have a deeper understanding and concern for her. She realised the conversation in the bedroom had moved on.

"Goodnight, my dears," said Mama now. "Sleep well and remember, no more arguments. It's Boxing Day tomorrow, and we'll have more fun after we've distributed the charity boxes at the hall."

I wonder if Michael will be there to help with that, Rose thought as her body sank and her conscious mind closed down.

CHAPTER 5

Easter 1914 came and went. It was time-consuming and expensive to return home. Rose spent the short vacation with a friend in the pretty downland village of Ashbury in the Vale of the White Horse, outside Oxford, so she didn't see Thom after all. Nor did she see Michael, but she thought of him often and hoped he was immersed in his course too. Another new term commenced. In May the students heard that the Balkan situation was still tense.

"The Turks were driven from southern Europe, but Bulgaria is far from happy with divisions of the land from the peace settlement and has decided to attack neighbouring Greece and Serbia. This second Balkan war seems to have resulted in Bulgaria losing further territory and the Serbs are becoming strengthened and revitalised," the Principal said one morning. "Girls, anyone, what will result from this?"

Rose was reluctant to put up her hand to reply, despite having discussed all this before she'd left for Oxford that first time. What if she were wrong? How foolish she would feel.

"Come along, girls. Miss Green, what do you think? You usually have something to say. Rose Strong, surely you can make a judgement." Miss Jex-Blake looked down the hall over her glasses.

Rose blushed and pushed her own spectacles up her nose. "It will leave the region of southern Europe politically unstable?" She spoke with a questioning inflection. "There is talk of war erupting because of the many and varied European alliances, I understand."

"Very good, Rose, exactly that."

Rose wrote to her papa about it, hoping to clarify her thoughts and relieve her fears.

My dear Papa,

I understand that Germany and Austria-Hungary are bound to each other and that A-H is already cross with Serbia after they voiced their objections to A-H annexing Bosnia-Herzegovina back in 1908. Papa, the Serbs had to support their people living in that region, did they not? Also, I read about Germany increasing their navy again *to match or even surpass ours, and they already have a good army. Is this correct?*

Do you consider this unrest in the Balkans will spread? France will not be happy with Germany, especially as she had part of her territory annexed with such ease during the 1870s Franco-Prussian war. You see I am discussing much here! I am worried that there will be a war and we shall be dragged into it because we have an understanding with France and Russia.

It would be terrible if Hector had to go and fight. He is so young and has not completed his studies.

I am trying hard to understand this situation, and Miss Jex-Blake has suggested we research and read all we can.

Please convey my love to the family. I miss everyone, even though I am enjoying my learning.

I remain your obedient (and hardworking) daughter,
Rose

Mr Strong's response to his daughter displayed undisguised pride at the hard work and insights she showed.

His letter gave family news, then she read:

My dearest daughter,
Do not fear. If there is to be a European war, it will be swift and will not involve Great Britain in any major way. Mr Asquith talked the other day

in the House of Commons and expressed similar sentiments to this.

While any war is terrible, recent wars have been swift to reach a conclusion. You mentioned the Franco-Prussian war which, once started, only lasted ten months. Both our own recent Boer wars in South Africa did not last long. There are technical advancements in recent years. Troops can be moved quickly using the railways, and those that start a conflict will be quick to use their guns so that a victor is decided rapidly.

If war comes to Europe, it will be over by Christmas and our great Country and Empire will be reluctant to become involved and probably will not have time anyway.

If you fear for your brother, there is no need. He is too young to fight. He will continue at the school until he has completed his studies. He was saying the other day that he might be interested in a college course too. I confess I was surprised since he does not fully apply the good brain that he has. I had a letter only the other day from his teacher to say that he spends more time chatting and gazing out of the window than he does studying his subjects. I daresay he will learn to concentrate better as he matures. I am sad that he does not work as hard as you do, dear daughter.

Keep up your studies in this way, dearest Rose, and you will learn well. You have an enquiring mind of which your mother and I are proud.

Please accept my fondest love,

Your proud Papa

The summer term at Oxford ran until the start of July. By this time, Rose had enjoyed many experiences and loved every minute of her time spent learning. Although her first love was literature, she unexpectedly found the history course interesting and her concern for current affairs was boundless. She devoured newspaper articles and stayed up late into the night debating and sharing views with her fellow students.

When she arrived home at the end of her first year, she thought Delphi and Izzy would believe her changed beyond their recognition. She was at pains to ensure she put them at their ease until the old camaraderie returned in full.

Izzy was her usual loving, loyal self. Delphi eventually relaxed into her habitual flamboyance, giving the impression of being carefree although Rose knew better. They saw little of Hector. He liked to be out and about with his friends. Rose noticed that he looked older than his years; he shaved and had broad shoulders, even though he was not yet tall.

"Delphi and Rose, please would you go to the Post Office for me? I need stamps and it's a lovely day for a walk. Izzy, you have your music lesson. Miss White will be here in half an hour."

Mrs Strong gave the money to Rose, who turned to find her jacket.

Rose and Delphi took the lane to the shop at the bottom of the town, rather than following the busier route where horses plodded and often dropped a load on the road. Halfway down the hill, they met Michael and Thom.

"Good morning, the Misses Strong," Michael said gallantly. "Where are you off to looking like a reflection of this beautiful summer's day?"

"Oh, Michael, you are such a flirt." Delphi laughed prettily. "We're just going to the little post office at the bottom of the hill. Mother needs postage stamps."

"It's not far and a lovely day for a little exercise," Rose added.

"Enjoy your walk," Michael said. "We may meet upon your return. Good day." The two boys touched their hats.

The girls continued on their way, but Delphi could not resist a backward glance, and neither could Rose. Just as she looked back, so did Michael.

"Oh no! He saw me looking." Rose felt herself colouring. She was mortified.

"He'll think you have a fancy for him now," Delphi teased her.

"Don't say that." Rose frowned at her.

They continued on their way pleasantly enough. They were sharing one of the rare times when, as sisters, they were friendly. The day was mild. Birds were loving the sunshine too and their singing in the hedgerow and up in the trees was joyful. Forget-me-nots sheltered under the greenery and the path was dusty with the lack of rain.

Halfway down the hill they stopped and rested their arms along the top of the five-barred gate and gazed across the wheat field. Here and there the corn was turning from blue-green to gold and poppies were showing their crimson. A lark arose close by. Its shrill singing made Delphi start, and both girls watched it until it became lost in the glare.

"How glorious," observed Rose with a contented sigh. "I might paint this afternoon. I could set up my easel just here and paint the landscape. Those misty lilac and blue hills make a beautiful backdrop to counter the colour of this wheat. The poppies make a good contrast."

"They are horrid flowers," Delphi said with feeling. "They remind me of blood and as soon as they are picked, they wilt and die."

"Oh Delphi, that is so sad. Then I shall paint bright buttercups instead and add cornflowers and chamomile. Yellows and blues would work just as well."

The girls left the lane and crossed the road, arriving at the little shop. Sheet tin advertisements for Nestlé's milk and Lipton's tea were pinned beneath the window. In the window itself were tins of cocoa powder, jars of sweets and packets of washing powder. As the sisters pushed open the door, the bell above clanged to announce their arrival.

"Good day, Mrs Goble," they greeted the customer who was already there.

Mrs Goble stood at the wooden counter having a gossip with the assistant post mistress. Her chins were wobbling and the flowers and cherries on her old-fashioned black bonnet were keeping time. Her short black cloak was edged with moth-eaten fur, and her full dark skirt was from a previous era too. She turned a rather sour face to the girls as they entered, unhappy to have such an interesting and scandalous conversation interrupted. "…that Kaiser, and he's our good King's cousin, too." Mrs Goble nodded her greeting, muttered something to the post mistress, tucked a strand of grey hair beneath her bonnet and left.

"Good morning." Rose addressed the lady behind the grille. "May we have half a dozen stamps, please?"

"Someone's doing a lot of letter-writing," the somewhat nosy post mistress stated.

The girls just nodded and smiled their response. Rose added, "It's a lovely day for a walk." She didn't want to appear rude, even though she had no desire to share any information in here. Having completed their purchase, the girls nodded their good-days and returned along the same route.

They had not gone more than halfway when they again met Michael and Thom.

"We meet again, ladies," Michael said, touching his tweed cap with two fingers in a mock salute.

"Well, Michael Redfern, you think yourself smart this morning," Delphi said, giving her light laugh which irritated Rose because it seemed so false. The camaraderie of earlier was dissipating fast.

"Good morning again." Rose nodded at the two boys. "Come Delphi, we must be on our way."

With that, the girls continued but to Delphi's delight and Rose's too, if truth be told, the boys followed them.

"What a lovely sight to behold," Thom said.

"A summer's day indeed," came the response.

"Truly beautiful," the conversation between the two lads continued.

Delphi and Rose exchanged glances and smiled at the other, irritations gone again.

The four continued along the lane towards the cut down to the girls' house, with the boys behind chattering to each other in similar vein.

"It's very warm, isn't it? I could do with a refreshing drink of lemonade." Michael started a new theme.

"It must be all this basking in such warm, reflected glory," added Thom. "I could do with something to drink too."

Delphi turned and said, "You better hurry along home, then."

Rose laughed at her sister's daring and gaining mirrored courage, she turned to the boys and added, "You two are outrageous."

"Not at all," Michael stated. "I'm simply commenting on the day. Of course, it is further to my house than yours so if you wanted to invite us in, we might not be able to resist." He smiled and the sun shone brighter still for Rose.

As the little entourage reached the spot where the path split, Michael tried one last time.

"I'm parched," he said and sighed. "Thom, you know, is a gentleman despite his roguish looks. He would be pleased to rest his leg."

"Michael Redfern, you are incorrigible," Delphi said, and she turned to face him with an impish look. "What do you think, Rose? Should we take pity on these rogues?"

"We shall have to," Rose responded, "or we might be responsible for a catastrophe beyond all reckoning. Far be it from us to deprive the young ladies of the town of the ongoing company of the likes of Michael Redfern." She grinned mischievously at her sister and then turned to the boys. "If you would care to join my sister and me, we might offer you a refreshing glass of lemonade before you pass away," she said.

Indoors, Dora huffed as she made her way around the kitchen, gathering glasses and a jug. "There's a luncheon to prepare, young ladies." The snowy pinafore covered her expansive frame and she swayed from side to side as she moved. Wispy slate-coloured hair was trying to escape from its pins, and her face was pink with exertion.

"Please would you bring the tray onto the terrace? Thank you, Dora, you are a dear." Rose gave her shoulder a gentle and affectionate pat.

As they sat with the lemonade, Delphi happily held court and the boys appreciated her chatter. She appeared to dismiss Thom quickly and turned her gaze to Michael, Rose observed. *Thom does nothing for her*, Rose thought. *Unlike Michael. She seems unable to resist teasing him for the confusion she obtains. She flirts with him all the time.* Rose tightened her jaw but managed to resist a sigh.

With deliberation, she sought to encourage the young man into the group conversations. "What about you, Thom? Have you got plans?"

"I'd like to study to be an engineer. There've been so many amazing inventions recently, especially with electricity."

"It's certainly changing things, but it seems scary to me," Delphi said and gave an affected little shudder.

"I'd love to invent something truly amazing," Thom said. Rose saw his eyes shining.

"You might end up with your name in lights, electric lights like Mr Faraday," Rose said.

"I'm thinking more of heavy engineering. My pa is trying to get me a place just east of Manchester at Adamson's at the Dukinfield works."

"Isn't that something to do with locomotive engines?" Rose asked.

Delphi was getting restless with so much attention being given to her sister and the others. She was unused to it and not a little resentful.

At dinner that night, Mr Strong said, "I passed young Michael Redfern and that friend of his, Thom. They appeared to be leaving."

"Yes, they were here for refreshment. We met them on the way back from the post office," Rose said.

"He's an intelligent young man is Michael," Mr Strong remarked. "We had a conversation about the European political situation. He is taking a good interest in affairs, and he reads sensibly without just regurgitating what he reads. He is thinking about it. I was impressed."

Delphi smiled, but it was Rose who said what she thought. "This present situation has its roots two years ago, in 1912, and even before that. I learned that Wilhelm II's opinion was that Austria should attack Serbia back then. If Russia supported the Serbs, which she evidently did, war would be unavoidable for Germany as an ally of Austria. He said at that time it would be a better option for Germany before Russia completed the massive modernization and expansion of their army they had begun."

"That's correct. I remember the Chief of the German General Staff was in favour of it too. He, Moltke, wanted to launch an immediate attack. That must be nearly two years ago now."

"So, since the incident of the murdered Archduke Franz Ferdinand at the end of June, they will be urging Austria to fight Serbia," Rose said.

"You have a good grasp of events, my dear."

Delphi asked, "I understand things are unsettled across there, but why Serbia?"

"The man who shot the Archduke and his wife is a Serbian, apparently," Mr Strong informed her.

"His wife was shot, too?" Izzy frowned. "That's horrible."

"Mr Strong…" Mrs Strong started to remonstrate about the tone of conversation at the dinner table.

"I know, my dear," he responded. "This is important, though."

"Is there to be a war?" Hector asked eagerly. "Will we get involved?"

"You are too young to fight abroad, anyway," Delphi said disparagingly. "You have to be nineteen. Isn't that right, Papa? You have to be eighteen to join up at all," she added.

"Yes, that is correct, Delphi. Anyway, Hector, even if Great Britain were to be involved, which is far from certain, it will all be over by Christmas, so you need not be excited about fighting anywhere," Mr Strong said firmly, glancing at his wife's anxious face.

"I gather that this Serbian, Gavrilo Princip, who shot the Archduke, is a member of a secret military society who wants to unify certain parts in the south of his country. I read that the

Serbian government made the gun he used for its own army, and that may give Austria an excuse to wage war. They are saying it is not just a small secret sect but the main government behind it." Rose spoke with concern.

"You and your college course; you seem to know it all," Delphi said waspishly.

"Now, children, enough talk of politics and fighting at the table. Eat your meal and let us hear no more of war now," Mrs Strong declared.

CHAPTER 6

The situation, in that summer of 1914, continued with demands from Austria-Hungary, partial compliance by Serbia and declarations of support for Austria-Hungary from Germany. Sir Edward Grey, for Great Britain, tried to ensure peace for the greater part of Europe by suggesting that Germany, France, Great Britain and Italy should act together but Germany declined, and even though Sir Edward met with the German ambassador separately the talks were not fruitful.

The Strong family took their customary summer vacation in the Yorkshire Dales with a day or two at the genteel resort of North Scarborough, where the girls donned their bathing dresses in a bathing hut and were wheeled into the sea to paddle.

"I'd like to visit the town, Papa. I should like to buy a memento of this place while we are all together here sharing a happy time. It looks like uncertainty ahead. It would be good to have a reminder of this holiday."

"A good idea, Rose," her father answered. "We shall walk down first thing in the morning."

During their evening meal, Mr Strong recounted what he had read in the newspaper that day.

"Russia began mobilisation of their forces ready to support their ally Serbia, but they are vacillating between fully and partially calling up their troops," he explained.

"It does not sound hopeful. I really do not like it," Mrs Strong remarked.

"Sir Edward Grey appealed to Germany to intervene to support peace. The British have informed their ambassador in

Germany, Sir Edward Groschen, that Germany contemplates war with France to settle old scores and the bad feeling that followed the Franco-Prussian war of the previous century. The Ambassador says they wish to send the German army through Belgium and asked for reassurance that Britain will remain neutral if such an action occurs," Mr Strong said. "The Germans really are being very belligerent, but it will not affect us unduly, my dear," he added when he saw the worried look on his wife's face.

The following morning, Rose said, "I think I might like to look in the window of Hutchens the jewellers, if I may."

Mr Strong accompanied Rose down the steep hill past the graveyard of St Mary's. They stopped for a moment and leaned on the wall to observe the gravestones.

Rose pointed. "Anne Brontë. Imagine her life and the writing she achieved. I loved her book *The Tenant of Wildfell Hall*."

The overhanging branches of the sycamore trees made it seem dark there and Rose shivered. They moved on and emerged into the sunshine again.

Having made their way into the town and to the shop they wanted, Rose looked at the beautiful gems and gold rings. Then she spied something quite different. It was advertised as a 'Fumsup Touch Wud'. The spelling alone was intriguing, but inside the box lid was a poem:

FUMS UP!
FOR LUCK

Behold in me
The birth of luck,
Two charms combined

TOUCH WUD — FUMSUP.
My head is made
Of wood most rare,
My thumbs turn up
To touch me there.
To speed my feet
They've cupid wings;
They'll help true love
'Mongst other things.
Proverbial is
My power to bring
Good luck to you
In everything.
I'll bring good luck
To all away —
Just send me to a friend today.

The little silver man lay on a card patterned with the Union Jack and was no more than one and a half inches tall.

"Oh, look, Papa, I should love to take a closer look at that," Rose said. "He is enchanting." The thought of owning this little talisman filled her with pleasure.

"These are all the rage, madam," said the obsequious salesman. "See here he has a four-leaf clover stamped into the front of his wooden head and it says 'Touch Wud' on the back."

"I can see the word 'Fumsup' on his little round tummy." Rose laughed gently.

"I do believe they will become more popular and valuable too, of course, if we start to send men abroad. They will be given to soldiers, I predict." The man bowed as he spoke and put his hands together in a submissive pose.

"You may be right, sir," Mr Strong said, "but we shall see if we send many soldiers to fight. Anyway, Rose, what do you think? Would you like this small fellow to remind you of a happy holiday?"

"I would indeed, Papa. He is delightful."

"This one in silver is 2 shillings and 4 pence, but we also have 9ct gold which is 12 shillings and 6pence, 15ct gold for 21 shillings or 15ct gold with real gem eyes the colour of your choosing for 30 shillings. I know it is a lot more, but of course it will only increase in value as I said before."

"I think we could take a gold one, my dear."

"Well, thank you, Papa, but I really like this little silver one with the natural eyes. He even has little pupils that seem to make his gaze follow me."

"Very well, dear child. He is yours."

Rose clutched her small parcel as they left the shop. Why did she feel this was so very special and different to previous gifts she had received?

The wheels of diplomacy trundled on, but by the end of July 1914 things looked increasingly dark. Britain asked both France and Germany to respect the neutrality of Belgium to which France acceded, but Germany did not respond.

Russia, France and Germany ordered general mobilisation. Austria-Hungary had already declared war with Serbia.

When Germany declared war with France and stated they would treat Belgium as an enemy if they did not allow passage of German troops across their land, they played an ace. Britain expected a German naval attack on the northern French coast, or so she said, and stated that she would give all the protection in her powers to France. On August 2nd, Asquith recognised that the Entente Cordiale of 1904 bound Britain to France (though much more loosely, in the eyes of most Britons, than France's view of the arrangement). Although Britain's obligation to Belgium stood, at this stage, he could not foresee Britain joining a continental conflict. Sealed allegiances had strength.

On August 4th, Britain didn't receive notification assuring the neutrality of Belgium. Germany invaded this country to approach French territory. Britain was forced to declare war in support of their ally France.

The family were nearing the end of their holiday when the news of this broke. Placards outside the newsagents' shops were full of it.

As the family entered the restaurant for their last evening, strains of 'Rule Britannia' could be heard somewhere outside followed by cheering and more singing.

"This is all quite exciting," Hector said, his eyes shining.

"I know," Delphi acknowledged. "I feel quite giddy."

"As I said the other day, children, it will not affect us unduly and will surely be over before it has begun."

Rose felt in her pocket for the little Fumsup Touch Wud she had bought. She moved his little arms with her finger surreptitiously until they touched its small wooden bead head.

Britain began a blockade of Germany, cutting off vital resources. Days passed. The family returned home and continued their lives. Declarations continued throughout the month, with the British, French and Russian Empires on one side, and the Germans and Austro-Hungarians on the other.

News was slow to filter through, but *The Manchester Guardian* and *The Times* informed the people.

"Since Austria invaded Russian Poland, Russia invades East Prussia and continues to make fast progress in the region through eastern Galicia," Mr Strong read one morning at breakfast.

The family followed Britain's progress as she fought the Battle of Mons and suffered huge losses but slowed the German advance whilst the First Battle of the Marne halted the German invasion of France. The Battle of Tannenberg shattered the Russian invasion and there were further losses at the Masurian Lakes.

At dinner one evening, Mr Strong recounted an incident of which he had heard. "One of our clients returned from Paris. He told us that the proprietor of the restaurant at which he dined said bluntly, 'Monsieur, if you have gold or silver, you may eat. If you have no gold or silver, you may leave.' Then he told us that rail travel from the city is impossible and the result is the most terrible congestion at the railway station."

"I must travel back to Oxford soon. The trains here are not like that, I hope," Rose said. "I cannot imagine how that must have been for your client. It is busy enough, is it not, Papa?"

"Indeed, Rose," he agreed. "I'm sure we shall have no trouble, though. The British Expeditionary Force has already left for France, and it is only four divisions who are travelling."

Shortly after, on a morning at the end of August 1914, the three Strong sisters walked through the main street of the town.

"It's such a relief to feel the breeze on my face," Delphi said. "It's been so hot for quite a while." She suddenly pointed up the street. "What on earth is going on over there?"

"There's a great crowd," Izzy said.

As they passed other shops, the same poster glared at them from many of the windows. It was about twelve inches tall and half as wide.

"That Union Jack background is striking," Rose observed with her artist's eye as she peered at the poster. "*YOUR KING and COUNTRY NEED YOU. ENLIST NOW.*"

"It's on the front of the *Daily Mail* and *The Times* too." Delphi pointed at the newspapers piled outside the shop next to which they stood.

"It's so horrid." Izzy hesitated as they moved further up the street to see what had happened.

The doors to the Salvation Army hall stood wide open and most of the crowd were young men. Rose spotted Michael and instantly she became aware of heat rising up her neck.

"Let's ask him what's going on." Delphi had seen him too and moved forward without hesitation. Rose delayed, but Izzy linked her arm then proceeded across the road in Delphi's wake to where Michael waited with the group of other men and boys.

"What's this? It's quite a crowd." Delphi nudged Michael's arm to get his attention, casually disregarding the appraising looks she got from the rest of the men.

"They are recruiting for the army to go and fight. It's exciting, the prospect of going abroad," Michael replied, eyes shining.

"But Michael, what about your teaching career?" Rose felt her brow crease with worry and horror and tried to relax her features. "And what of your parents? What have they said?"

"Mother's not happy at all. She's worried, I know, but my father understands. He told me I'm only young once, and it's a grand adventure. His money won't be wasted. He knows I'll go back to teaching when I return. This is for King and Empire, and it won't last long," he responded assuredly. "I can complete my college course later."

"You are so brave." Delphi smiled up at him.

"Will you visit and tell us about it before you leave?"

"Yes, Izzy, I'll call if I am able," Michael assured the youngest of the sisters.

The crowd, which the girls could see was a long queue, moved forward. Michael had to enter the hall with the next group.

Rose wanted to press her Fumsup Touch Wud into Michael's hand, but she dared not be so forward. She shuddered without knowing why.

As they left, the girls were quiet and even Delphi was thoughtful.

"I wanted to buy ribbon to decorate my straw hat," Izzy said. "I think I'll leave it for another time. Maybe I'll get red, white and blue ribbons now. That would be fetching and patriotic too," she added, brightening.

CHAPTER 7

Michael entered the hall with friends from his father's store and one or two others with whom he had been to school.

"Name? Age?" Michael was asked this abruptly as he reached the head of the queue and notes were made about him in a large lined book.

"Right, over there and strip off," a medic said.

"Stand here," another said. His height was measured, and his weight taken.

"Bloody 'ell! It's dusty in 'ere, lads. Clouds of it," one lad said.

The wooden floor was filthy from the hundreds of boots that had already trodden there.

"Stinks an' all," said another.

The musty smell from so many men filled the hall. Only the sky with patches of clear blue and shining clouds could be seen through the high windows. The walls were beige and dull.

"That'll do, that'll do," a fellow in uniform said. "'Ere, you, to that table over there, and you lad, at the next one, there."

Michael moved towards the table. A screen made from shabby cotton fabric with stripes of red and dingy green stretched over metal frames only gave minor privacy. Several officers in khaki uniforms and big boots strode about the hall looking important. Between the metal and the material of the screens could be seen men and boys sitting in various stages of undress. The medical personnel examined some, listening to their chests with stethoscopes, looking down throats using wooden spatulas or feeling glands around necks. Peering around the screen at the table to which he was pointed,

Michael surveyed an army medic seated, metal dishes and jars of wooden spatulas in front of him.

"Let's have you," the medic said. "Open wide."

After that, Michael was told to go through to the next room.

"What's next?" The lad next to him seemed wary.

"Get the rest of yer kit off. Look lively," a soldier said.

In his underwear Michael stood and waited. The skinny lad ahead of him stood with hunched shoulders and arms folded over his scrawny chest.

"And the rest. Don't be a girly. We're in this together," the soldier said.

Stark naked, Michael was asked to walk back and forth, embarrassed as he moved. He became more so as his body parts were examined, and he was asked to cough. Then came relief when told to get dressed.

"You ready for glory, sonny?" Someone in uniform approached him and asked the question.

"Yes, sir, absolutely, sir," Michael responded.

"How old are you?"

"Eighteen, sir. I shall be nineteen in October, though."

"You'll do. By the time you've done yer training, you'll be what we need. 'Ere, sign this for the King's shilling and stand over there."

A group of men, including Michael, stood to take the oath of allegiance.

"Come back 'ere at four o'clock and we'll go."

"Thank you," Michael responded. "Excellent!"

Once outside again in the sunshine, he waited for his friends. When they were together, there was much chatter and excitement.

"I can't wait," one said. "All that French wine and mademoiselles for the asking."

"Give me the chance for a bit of glory," said another. "What about you, Michael? What are you looking forward to most?"

He blew out his cheeks. What he had done suddenly hit him, but he wouldn't show any doubt in front of the others. "Well, lads, give me the chance to stick it to them."

They laughed uproariously. It was such a relief to laugh out loud together.

The girls wandered desultorily, looking in shop windows.

"I think we might as well go home," Rose said.

Delphi jumped in quickly. She had no wish to return yet. "Izzy, I want to go and buy some cold cream. I heard there is a new range at Redfern's. Elizabeth Croft was telling me about it when she and her mama came for tea the other day. Will you come with me?"

Izzy raised her eyebrows. "You don't normally want my company," she said.

"Well, now I do, but if you're going to be like that…"

"No, no, I'll come, please. I'd like some more green thread for my sampler as well as that ribbon," Izzy said happily enough. "It would be nice to stay out a bit longer. I do nothing but sew, practise the piano and my declensions for Frau Schröder. I do love the German language, though, and I'm very lucky to have a native speaker to teach me."

"I don't understand the compulsion for academia in this family. It is so unnecessary. What use will it be when we marry? It will not be appreciated. It is much more important to have wifely skills and be able to run a household. You only have to look around at the houses of Mama's friends. A happy husband is a happy family."

"Papa says the future of this country will rely on the learning of our generation — girls and boys," Izzy said.

"That's his opinion, but it won't make babies and feed the family. I want a husband who is dashing and brave and will give me a comfortable home. He will earn a pile and I shall dress like a princess. I shall cherish and look after his every need."

Izzy asked, "Rose, are you coming?"

"Huh! Rose won't want to stay out any longer. She has more of her precious college work to do before the new term commences," Delphi said.

"Delphi's correct, I do have an essay to finish and some Latin translation to do before I return to college, and I would like to go home and share all that we have learned with Mama too."

It was not far to Redfern's Department Store to make their purchases.

"There's Michael!" Izzy exclaimed.

"You're such a little innocent, Izzy."

Izzy hesitated and looked at the radiant face of her sister. The knowledge dawned and she frowned. "Delphi! You knew he would be coming here."

"So what? I do indeed need some face cream."

"Mmm, right."

Michael headed towards the main door but stood to one side to wait for them to catch up. Delphi admired his height and physique. He was broad-shouldered and his legs were long and sturdy.

"Good day again, Delphi, Izzy," he said as they all arrived at the door together.

"Michael, what a surprise!" Delphi spoke artlessly, looking up at him and using her most dazzling smile.

There was a discreet 'tch' from Izzy and Delphi turned with a cold stare.

"Izzy, dearest, why don't you pop in and buy your thread? I'll catch up with you shortly when Michael and I have exchanged news."

"Very well, Delphi, but don't be long, will you, *please*?"

As she went, Delphi added, "She's such a poppet but still so young. How are you, Michael? Did you sign the paper and take the King's shilling?"

"I did, and we're off for training next. I need to see my parents before we leave this afternoon. We shall be using bayonets and doing close contact combat. It's exciting, but I want to get over to France before it's too late."

"Of course you do. We're all so proud of you." Delphi touched his arm lightly with the tips of her fingers and smiled up through her lashes.

"Delphi, I was wondering if you would write to me while I'm away. It would be so lovely to get news of you all and the places here that I love so much."

"Of course I shall. It would help us to be close while you are away. I shall cheer you with my idle chatter," she answered.

"I shall miss everyone."

"You are so brave."

"I haven't had the chance to be brave yet, but I hope I will be when the time comes."

"You will," she said. "You will be my dashing hero and sweep the entire enemy away just for me. I shall be here waiting for you when you return."

Michael looked uncomfortable, but ever gallant he smiled down at her and said, "You are a sweet child."

"But I'm not a child, Michael," she said with a degree of vehemence. "I have the heart of a woman and I shall be here for you, my brave, conquering hero."

"Delphi, how old are you now, seventeen?"

"I'm nearly eighteen."

"Not for six months."

"So? Age is irrelevant. It's experience and understanding that count," she said.

He smiled.

Huh, he thinks me innocent. He probably thinks I don't realise what he will be doing, she thought.

"Well, *I'm* too young," he said. "I have much to achieve and a college course to complete before I settle down. Anyway, changing the subject," he continued, "how is Rose getting on at her college? I must ask Rose to write too."

"Oh, Rose! It's all about Rose in our house. Clever Rose with her talk about current affairs and Miss Jex-Blake said this and Miss Jex-Blake said that. All she and Papa discuss is college talk. I tell you, Michael, it is dull, dull, dull! She doesn't seem fun at all anymore. You will find her extremely changed."

Delphi tossed her hair and pouted in what she hoped was a replica of Mary Fuller, about whom she had read. The article in *The Guardian* that Papa had left open next to his breakfast plate was about her nomination for one of the top three silent movie stars of 1913, and the photograph showed long dark hair and full lips.

"Don't be envious of Rose and her brains. You are a special person too."

"So, you do love me a little bit?" Delphi pressed his arm with her fingers and searched his face for deeper meaning.

Michael smiled gently and laughed down at her. "Oh, Delphi, we are far too young to speak of love. I have no intention of loving anyone for years. Now come along and let's find Izzy and stop all this nonsense."

He turned and Delphi's eyes stung. She lifted her chin, however, and marched next to him, sweeping in through the door that he held wide for her.

Rose descended the stairs at the sound of her sisters' return. "Did you make your purchases?"

"Yes, thank you, Rose," Izzy said. "We saw Michael Redfern again, too." She took off her jacket, unpinned her hat and placed them on a chair in the hall. With that, she headed for the day room with her new thread.

Rose watched her go. "What did he have to say?"

"Come upstairs with me, Rose, and I'll tell you while I sort these outdoor clothes," Delphi said.

They climbed the wide stairs companionably.

"He's off for training straight away," Delphi divulged.

"We won't see any of them for a while." Rose sighed, causing Delphi to look more closely at her.

"I suppose that's true."

Rose cast her eyes down and turned away. She did not want Delphi to read her desperate expression, but when she glanced across at her sister, she saw Delphi's scrutiny.

Delphi took a deep breath. "He told me he loves me, you know."

Rose spun round. She couldn't help it. It was a reflex action.

Delphi turned towards the armoire with her jacket in her hand, but as she did Rose saw an expression of triumph. *She knows I cannot best her in this*, she thought. "I'm surprised he has time to consider such things," she said aloud.

"Oh, yes. I've known for some time how he felt, but we're not sharing it with anyone else. You must tell no one, Rose. I'm entrusting only you with this most important of secrets. At least he will have some dreams to take away with him." Delphi was really getting into the swing of the story now. "I gave him my handkerchief and he placed it in his pocket — next to his heart. It's so wonderful to be adored."

"I see, yes, of course."

"Come, let us find Izzy, and maybe Dora will have something for us to eat. I'm famished." With that, she breezed out of the door, leaving Rose sitting on the bed.

Rose lay back on the pillows and curled up her legs. She did not cry. She was numb. *I suppose I was aware all along that it would be Delphi he adored.* She had seen how his eyes had sought and followed her enigmatic and beautiful sister.

How could I have ever considered he might like me as more than a friend? He has always been kind and polite. I remember he thought I would be interested to see the Cathedral at Peterborough. He gave me the handkerchief and had found one with a small rose in the corner. He was being gallant and kind, that's all.

She gave an enormous sigh and sat up.

But Delphi is too young for him, and not only in years. She does not think deeply as he does. She is so vain and ... and ... oh, I don't know!

With that, she raised her foot and kicked out at the chair next to the bed.

Immediately she was remorseful. Self-pity was stupid and pointless. She must throw herself into her studies and do the best that she could there. She loved the challenge of intellect and when this awful war was done, she would teach others and show young people the joy of learning.

CHAPTER 8

When Rose went downstairs, the atmosphere gave no pretence of light-heartedness.

"Is something amiss, Mama?" Rose could see the worried look on her mother's face.

"It's Hector," Mrs Strong said. "He's gone missing. I haven't seen him all morning. He wasn't in his room when I went up and knocked, and he is nowhere to be found. I sent Dora to your father's work. He has explained to his employers that Hector has disappeared and he has gone to look for him."

Tears welled, and Rose went to put her arm around her mother's shoulders.

"Has he gone to join the army?" Delphi went straight to the point. "He can't do that; he's not old enough."

"No, he's not." Her mother wiped her eyes and lifted her head. "Papa will find him," she added with a confidence she did not feel.

Half an hour later, Mr Strong returned to the house. "I went to the recruiting hall in the town and asked if he had gone there to join up," he said.

Mrs Strong gasped and put her hand to her mouth. "Do you think he might have done that?"

"They wouldn't tell me. They said I'd need proof of his age, and after that it might be possible to retrieve any document he might have signed."

"Oh, no! This is a nightmare," Mrs Strong cried out.

"I wish we had seen fit to get birth certificates for our children," Mr Strong said to his wife. "It is not the norm, but it could have proved that he's not old enough for enlistment."

"He's nowhere near the age for going overseas. What shall we do?" Mrs Strong's voice rose in panic.

A heavy silence descended as both parents contemplated the issue.

"Why don't you go and speak to Reverend Johns? He will have records of when he christened Hector," Rose said.

"Yes, he will write a letter stating his age and you can take it to the recruiting hall." Mrs Strong grasped her husband's arm in her urgency.

"I shall go now with the utmost haste." He rushed off, leaving his family to comfort each other.

As they waited, Mrs Strong became more and more agitated, and Rose did her best to calm her. Izzy was in a similar state and Delphi, unsure how to cope, had departed to her bedroom to read, although Rose guessed she would sit and stare out of the window.

Some time later, Mr Strong returned. As soon as they heard the door, they rushed to the hall. He waved a paper.

"I have got the document stating that Hector is too young and that he will not join the others when they march out later. They are leaving at four o'clock this afternoon. We shall never discover where he is hiding before that, but we shall be able to pick him out as they go."

"What if we can't find him or he joins the file somewhere out of town?" asked Mrs Strong.

"The officers will spot him, and I shall be there too. We shall get him back, my dear. Do not fret. They go to Manchester first for training. We will be able to find him there, if not today."

Three o'clock came and Mrs Strong was in no fit state to go anywhere, but Mr Strong and Rose put on their jackets to go into the town.

"We shall walk rather than wait for the motor omnibus. It will be quicker in the long run, but we must hurry."

"Yes, Papa," answered Rose.

"Don't go without me," Delphi said. "I'm not missing any of this. I want to cheer our boys and watch Michael Redfern and his friends when they leave. He said he would come by here, but he hasn't."

"Don't be peevish," Rose said to her. "I expect he hasn't had time. Anyway, our aim is to find Hector."

"I know, I know," Delphi replied as she rammed in her hat pin.

Rose saw her peek in the hall mirror. "Delphi, do come," Rose said, and Delphi ran to catch up with her sister and father.

When they arrived in the small town centre there was a heaving, surging mass of humanity lining the road, many of whom waved small flags. Ever speedy to exploit a situation, Mr Richards from the newsagent shop sold them and made a brisk trade.

"I must find a senior officer," Mr Strong said. "Girls, stay together and wait for me here."

"Can you see anyone, any of the lads?" Delphi asked Rose, who couldn't see much of anything except people's arms waving and heads bobbing to get a better view of the road. "I wonder where Michael is."

"Delphi, we need to keep watch for Hector."

"Yes, that too."

From up the street the girls heard a band play. The penny whistles were the most melodious, but Rose picked out trumpets and drums too. Although the sound was not strong, it was jolly and had she not been worrying for her brother,

Rose would have been carried along with the mood of the rest of the crowd.

"Can you see him? Scan the crowd, look along the road. We must watch as they pass," Rose said to her sister. She craned her neck and peered around as best she could, increasingly frustrated and worried.

"Michael won't be passing yet," Delphi said.

"Oh, Delphi, for goodness' sake! Not Michael, Hector. We must watch out for Hector." Rose could not keep the exasperation from her voice.

There was a frisson of excitement and pride. Then a mighty roar arose from the crowd. Mothers looked for sons and shouted names as they were spotted. Wives wept and called to husbands, trying to sound brave.

Here was adventure and tingling self-importance mixed with trepidation and expectation personified in the column of men who tried so hard not to appear like a rag-tag band of misfits as they marched along the centre of the road.

Rose spotted Michael.

"He's there," Delphi shouted as she, too, saw him. "Michael, hurrah!"

"Delphi, please," Rose said, but as he turned she waved at him.

Did he give a wink? Rose was unsure, but she had a rush of breathlessness and a surge of heartbeats.

In the next moment she felt a traitor to her own brother. She had forgotten to scan the road for him. What if she had missed him?

Michael wouldn't have been winking at me, she thought. *It's Delphi for whom he is all eyes.*

As the column passed, the people on the pavements experienced a sense of collective deflation. Silence settled like a mist and people turned away with heads lowered. Rose did the same.

"Well, I suppose that's it. Hector has gone. We may never see him again," she said to Delphi.

"I'm sorry, Rose. I should have tried harder to find him in the column."

"We must wait here for Papa now. I cannot imagine what Mama will say."

"This is so foolish; we might be here for…" Delphi paused as she spotted two figures. "Papa … and Hector!"

Rose turned. Her father approached with Hector, who was looking cross. She hurried towards them.

"The prodigal returns," Mr Strong said, looking at his glowering son. "Come along now. Home we go to share the glad news with your mother, and you shall hear the whole sorry story."

"I cannot believe Hector scared us like that," Delphi said to Rose once they were home and in Delphi's bedroom.

"As he said to Papa, he feels strongly about the rights and wrongs of the political situation." Rose justified his views for Izzy to understand too. "He has been brought up since early childhood to believe in heroes. Indeed, he is named for one. In the Boy Scouts and in school he has learned to be brave and heroic."

"But he's not old enough," Izzy said.

"That's true, poppet, but he is excited by the atmosphere without understanding the implications. Many are going for the adventure. Some may even go for full square meals each day and shoes upon their feet."

"What do you mean?"

"Well, Izzy, not everyone is as fortunate as we are. You've seen some of the lads playing in the streets, and you know Mama took baskets of food to Mrs Robertshaw in River Lane when her husband was laid off. Not everyone can afford proper food or boots for the younger ones," Rose explained.

"Really, Hector should have known better than to worry us," Delphi said.

"Yes, like you were so worried!" Rose couldn't resist having a dig at her.

"I was. When Papa told us how that Corporal found him falling in with the others, it was such a relief. It shows how naïve he is to do that. Of course he would be discovered."

"That's true, but I imagine he wanted a tiny share of the glory they received, and he got carried away with it."

"What will happen now? Will he be in real trouble?"

"I am unsure, Izzy," Rose answered. "I imagine Mama and Papa will discuss that, but Papa will sit and talk with him and explain why it's impossible for him to go to war at his age. Now, I must go and find Dora and remind her to make sure my grey dress is ready. I only have a few days before I must start packing again."

"I shall miss you, Rose," Izzy said.

"It won't be long until I return at Christmas," Rose reassured her youngest sister. "We should be getting back to normal by then," she added with optimism.

As it turned out, Rose did see Michael again before she left for Lady Margaret's.

The lads' initial training was in Manchester and they came home each night, so it was only a few days later when Rose met him. She was on her way to the village shop when Michael was returning from the very same place.

Whilst she felt her face heating with pleasure, in the next moment Rose also wished the ground would swallow her. It was her sister for whom he had declared his love. She did not want to see or hear the evidence of this with her own eyes. Yet she could not resist poking the wound.

"Michael, I hear you are having more training and may be moving."

"Mother is still distressed about me joining up."

"I imagine you will soon be sad to be going further away and leaving the people you love."

"To be honest, Rose, nothing feels very different. We have been continuing to live at home; I have no proper uniform or anything. I think we're all pleased to be getting on with it, even if it means moving away."

"And others? Other people will miss you too." Rose couldn't resist probing.

"Oh, you know; a mixture of emotions, I suppose. I was wondering if you would write to me while I am away, Rose."

"Write to you? Me? Well, yes, of course." She felt the warmth rising again.

"I shall miss here and the people in the village. You have an artist's eye and will be able to tell me of the little things that matter so much; this lane, where we have met before and shared happy times, the flowers in the hedgerow, the colours of the fields which are my home. You can give me scraps of news and tell me your thoughts."

She saw his eyes, his piercing summer blue eyes, looking closely at her.

"You have perception for these small things, and it would mean much to me, Rose."

She smiled up at him with genuine joy and felt her heart lurch. "It would be a delight to cheer you up with small snippets. You are off on a grand adventure. It's a good thing while you have the chance, but do be careful and stay safe. As your friend I shall miss you. I know Delphi will too."

"Oh Rose," he said but then no more, leaving her wondering.

Having said his goodbyes to Rose, Michael walked on in a pensive mood.

Her replies to his request had been so different from Delphi's. She seemed to grasp that he was not yet ready to settle down.

I can't think of romance when there is a war to be fought. Rose knows this. She has lovely eyes behind those glasses and her figure is neat too, but she doesn't display it in such an attention-seeking way as Delphi.

CHAPTER 9

"I can't believe we're in the 4th City Pals of the Manchester Regiment," Michael said to Bertie. "Doesn't it sound grand?"

"At least we're together," Bertie replied. "It'll make the whole adventure much greater, sharing it."

They weren't close friends, but they knew each other from school days. They had different backgrounds, but Michael was easygoing and happy to be friends with almost anyone. Bertie's mother had brought up him and his four siblings with little material or emotional help. What money came in was sporadic and was frequently spent down at the pub. For Bertie, this was an opportunity to have three good meals each day and maybe soon a set of clothes that were his alone.

"Blimey, it's good to have a break from all those hours of drill we've been doing."

"It doesn't seem much like an adventure, though, does it?" said Michael. "Here we are, September already, doing drill but we've still got our own clothes. I want to wear a uniform. I want to look the part. And going home each night; it's not like we're in the army."

"You want to dress up and charm the girls, do you?" Bertie smirked at him. "Well, we should get something soon. I 'eard that so many joined up they couldn't keep up wiv it, 'specially since the uniforms the regular army 'ad before were made in Germany, so that source has dried up." Bertie laughed at the idea. "Eh, that's a turn up innit? Our army's uniforms made by Jerry an' now they can't get 'em for love nor money." He chuckled again.

"Belle Vue has never seen this, I bet," Michael observed as he gazed across the Manchester ground at the dozens of men practising with their wooden guns, awaiting the real thing. "This is slightly ridiculous. Wooden rifles. My own clothes. No barracks. All we're doing is marching for eight hours. I want to go and kill the enemy."

"It's not that easy keeping in step though, is it?"

The following week they did receive uniforms. The people of Manchester donated nearly twenty-seven thousand pounds to clothe their boys as soldiers.

"Navy blue!" remarked Michael. "But the red piping sets it off, I suppose."

"What do I look like in this 'ere cap? It's like a marine's with its peak." Bertie struck a pose. "Can you picture me with a pint in me 'and? I'll get me women now, don't you think? Delphi Strong will be all over you like a rash now an' all, except you don't want a rash." He laughed at his own wit.

"Mind your mouth, Bertie. Mmm." Michael was thoughtful for a moment. "Do you remember, after that Jewish bloke was taken aside? The talk from the magistrate after we touched the Bible and made the oath of allegiance to the King? Wine, women and song, he said. Beware, he said. Remember? He sounded so severe with his gruff voice and those huge great whiskers. What a lecture he gave us. Scared me half to death, it did."

"Yeah, well, he's too ancient to have the energy. Not like us gallant boys, eh?"

It wasn't long before arrangements altered, and the new troops moved to Heaton Park where they were billeted in tents before constructing their own huts as winter approached.

Before the war started, the historic parkland had always been a favourite with families and as autumn turned colder and the leaves dropped from the trees there were often visitors among the amateurish military. Bright dresses and hats with feathers contrasted with the stark living accommodation of the men and the muddy ground around their bell tent entrances.

Towards the end of December 1914, the Strong family accompanied Mr and Mrs Redfern on one such outing. Rose was relieved and pleased to accompany them, having finished another term at Lady Margaret Hall.

"This is so exciting," Delphi said. Her cheeks flushed with the cold and the thrill of the adventure. She was as radiant as she had ever looked. The peacock feather in her royal blue hat bobbed as she twisted with a little skip to address the families.

"It's all so busy and noisy," Izzy said. "How will we manage to find anyone at all?" She turned her head in haste and moved closer to her mother as an officer shouted to a group of troops nearby.

"I am so proud of these men," Rose said. "They are putting their lives on hold and giving up so much to guard our safety."

"You are absolutely right, my dear," agreed Mr Strong.

Rose shivered. The air was chill, but it wasn't that which caused her to tremble as she surveyed the scene. She felt a frisson of fear for these lads, many of whom were no older than she.

There were four main camps in the park. Having entered by the Bury Old Road entrance, the two families made their way with caution.

"So noisy. Such a banging and a hammering. What a mountain of beams and planks," Mrs Strong remarked.

Izzy moved to accompany her brother. They walked together, heads bent, but he seemed to be barely listening to her prattle. His eyes roamed from one side to the other, taking it all in. Mrs Strong recognised the expression of envy on her beloved son's face.

"While my mind understands his eagerness, my heart is so thankful that he's still too young to enlist," she said to Mrs Redfern.

"I do so understand that, Mrs Strong. Michael is hellbent on serving the King and Empire. It's commendable, but I do worry." She sighed.

"There are so many here," Delphi said. "We shall never find him." She sounded exasperated.

"I am sure we will see him soon," Rose said calmly. "We are in the right area now, and Mr Redfern seems confident." She glanced at her sister's flushed complexion and inside she shrank. *I wish I had half her beauty. Her hair is always sleek and lovely, and even with this cold wind she still manages to look elegant and not in the least like an apple. I'm just a ragamuffin with my flyaway hair, and I imagine my cheeks have gone red with the chill*, she thought.

Everywhere those not directly involved in building huts were marching, inclining, turning at the double, and forming fours and squads; the sound of boots was at odds with the beating of hammers.

In the distance they spotted another group performing a physical drill, bodies ramrod straight, arms and legs extended and yet another group running, running, running while someone bellowed at them to keep together.

Then they saw Michael and his company as they performed a drill manoeuvre.

"He's there, he's over there!" Delphi grabbed Rose's arm in a vicelike grip and pointed with her other hand.

"Delphi, restraint, if you please," her mother chided. "She's still so young," she added to Mrs Redfern, who nodded with understanding.

They stood and watched. Rose's heart pounded at the sight of him, so tall and distinctive in his navy-blue uniform. He looked so broad-shouldered and handsome. She strained to control her breathing and expression. She had seen Thom a few times and they had been on outings, but he never had this effect on her.

Eventually they observed the instructions from an officer to fall out. Michael saluted and had a quick word with his sergeant before heading towards them. He greeted his parents, shook Mr Strong's hand and then inclined his head to the rest of the company. His eyes danced among them and then focused on Delphi and her loveliness.

"Still in navy blue, then, son," Mr Redfern said. "Still getting called the 'tram guard'?"

"Yes," Michael said and frowned. "It's not appreciated, I can tell you. When there was talk of us moving before, we hoped it would be to France, and here we are just across the city."

"Well, you play the part of a brave soldier to me," Delphi said, earning a frown from her mother which she shrugged away carelessly.

"You'll get your khaki in good time, I'm sure," said Mrs Redfern. "Are they feeding you properly now you are living here?"

"Oh yes, porridge and toast this morning with two cups of tea and plenty of sugar, mother." He smiled at her before his eyes were drawn back to Delphi, who smiled up at him.

She's willing him to look at her, I bet, thought Rose. *How can she be so obvious? It's pathetic!* She sighed. *He's mesmerised, bewitched. Delphi is enchanting.* Her thoughts turned uncharacteristically churlish. *I cannot be like that. It'd not be true to me. Flirting so noticeably is too silly.*

By March 1915 there was talk of the 19th Manchester Battalion, as the 4th City Pals had become known, moving to Grantham for further training.

Michael was frustrated. "When the hell are we going to get across there and give them the fecking drubbing they deserve? This war will be longer than first thought, judging by Mons."

"We were far outnumbered there, and the retreat was bloody, but we've put a stop to them at the Marne and their Schlieffen plan is in disarray," one of the others, now a private, said.

"We've protected Paris. I don't want to miss the fun. It'll be over before we get there," Michael said to his friends.

"Yes, you're right. When we get to Grantham, we might get our khakis and start real training instead of this drill. That'll be better."

"Let's 'ope it's not for long and we can really get going," Bertie said.

"We've got leave coming up before Grantham. That'll distract you, but I know what you mean," the private offered.

"What'll you do then, Michael? Me, I think I'll sleep for a whole day and then go down the pub. I'll not drink all me pay, though. Not like me Da, but it'll be good to show the old 'uns what we soldier boys are made of, eh?"

"Yes, leave will be good," Michael said.

"'Ave you got a girl to see?"

"I could have if I wanted, I believe," he responded.

CHAPTER 10

January 1916

Rose lifted her skirts as she descended into the hall. She could not help glancing at the salver on the table at the bottom of the stairs as she did each day, in hope. There lay a letter, small and thin, with the censor's franking stamp she had seen but once. She snatched it up and glanced around the hall. She had no wish to share Michael's news until she had read it several times herself.

"What are you up to?" Delphi asked as she came downstairs. "You look like the proverbial cat with the cream."

"Nothing, Delphi, dear." She drifted towards the dining room, slipping the letter into her pocket.

Although Michael had asked her to write while he was away, it was no time before she discovered he had also asked Delphi. Of course he had. He loved her, didn't he?

Michael had not been away long when he sent Rose and her sisters each an embroidered postcard. Izzy's card was sweet with birds and flowers, and on Delphi's flags were picked out in satin stitch with a message that said 'Souvenir from France' in colourful thread. Rose did not know whether Delphi had responded, although her youngest sister had asked for a message of thanks to be included in Rose's tin of cake. The card for Rose had the Manchester's regimental badge with its rampant lion and antelope supporting the shield so full of symbolism. The inscription read '*Concilio et Labore.*' Rose understood this meant 'Wisdom and Effort'. Underneath, two embroidered roses lay in a beautiful shade of pink.

She placed her own card on top of the handkerchief in a box in her drawer.

Dear Rose,

I am so happy that you said that we could correspond. As a friend, you said, but a friend is a rare treasure indeed, for us soldiers abroad.

When we last met, I was proud that you and your sisters saw me in my 2nd Lieutenant's uniform. My teacher training has stood me in good stead. Even though my time at college was short, the promotion indicates they seem to think I can manage this lot. Those last sessions at Grantham and then on Salisbury Plain taught me much about the observation skills I shall need as a ground scout for the Battalion. I learned map and compass use and all about listening and reporting too.

When I saw you, I had such a confusion of feelings. I was part tunic, puttees, badges and Webley revolver and part nervous, self-conscious boy. Then again, I felt a lightning burst of excitement on the one hand and a deep and desperate sadness at leaving on the other.

Getting rid of the navy blue 'tram drivers' gear in favour of this new uniform was a relief, to be honest. We were grateful to the people of Manchester for buying us a proper uniform back then, but I am happy to be wearing the King's khaki now. I'm not being vain but proud to represent my King and Empire.

We crossed the Channel on the SS Queen Alexandra. When we landed, the countryside was exactly like that which we'd left. It looks no different, yet we are in a foreign country. Then we coped with a train journey in which we loaded thirty men into each cattle truck. There was no room to sit and the smell was dreadful. Since then we have marched and marched. I am not allowed to tell you where, Rose.

As an officer (of sorts!), they detailed me to chivvy the stragglers. I managed to commandeer ambulances for those whose blisters made them lame. By the time we'd skidded around in the mud and arrived at our destination, I was ready to drop like a stone into my bed. I've hardly had time to notice the surrounding countryside abroad and cannot believe it.

I am learning much about commanding men while on the job; a fresh-faced lad compared to many of the chaps in my patrol. I don't want them to think I'm a know-all, but they will not give respect because I wear a leather belt and they do not. We are a Pals Battalion and have joined up together to be with friends. I must command and give them courage and discipline. I must be decisive and efficient. It's hard when I still feel their equal. I must hide that at all costs and be friendly but not friends. Still, I can leave the harsh stuff to the CO, who is regular army.

The weather is depressingly wet and heavy. The clouds are thick, making it dark even during the day. Our billets are lousy and the local estaminet, a café, is greasy and grey, but despite everything we are optimistic. This morning I am bursting with energy and tumultuous spirit as we await further movement forwards. I still cannot hear the guns and I have a marvellous enthusiasm to get going.

I must go now and rouse my platoon. Thank you for the cake, Rose. Your parcel and the note from Izzy lifted my spirit when I was so tired the other day. At least the postage service is first rate and we are getting letters and parcels in good order and promptly.

Please give my best regards to your parents and to Hector and your sisters.

Very best wishes
Michael

"Let's be at it, boys. Stand to, now. Rum ration after this, so look lively," Michael told his men. "Here're the duties for today." He started with the rota. "John, you and Bertie collect the cartridge cases and put them into a sandbag."

John was a young fresh-faced lad with blond hair and fluff on his top lip. He'd been a quiet, sheltered schoolboy before enlisting. He insisted he had been at college too, but Michael doubted he was old enough. He had teamed John up with the more confident and world-wise Bertie and quietly told him to watch out for the lad.

"You three are on sentry duty this morning. For Christ's sake, don't forget the gas gong if there's any sign. You others are pumping water. This rain's a bugger in the trenches and we've had so much of it."

"'Ere sir, 'ave we got bacon again for breakfast?" Bertie nudged his mate, Ben. "Bloody good that were yesterday." These were two big, bluff and red-faced men who understood hard work, even if Ben pretended otherwise.

"Make the most of it, Bertie. It'll be bread and butter before you know it. Right men, get those rifles cleaned and ready for inspection."

The next four days passed in routine order before they were relieved at midnight by the 2nd Wiltshire Regiment.

"We're pulling back to Billon Wood, to be support to the firing line," Michael told his platoon. "We'll be doing mining fatigues."

"Bloody 'ell, sir."

"Enough of that, Ben. You need to work off those breakfasts you've been stuffing."

The men on this duty carried away the sandbags full of dirt the miners dug. It was a heavy, filthy task, but not as dangerous as the work the miners did as they dug tunnels and laid explosives under the enemy trenches. Every so often, their work came to an abrupt halt as they listened to the other side digging similar tunnels.

"Them miners are 'ard lads," Bertie said one morning.

"They seem to be short, tough men who don't say much," Ben answered.

"Have you seen that fellow, Jenkins? He's like Hercules. He's huge. His neck's like a bull and he can sink a pint from what I heard." John, the youngster, spoke in awe. He was unused to rubbing shoulders with these taciturn men.

After several turns of these activities, the men had to march six miles to the new location. It was not a marching battalion as Michael had seen at home. Oh no. They staggered in groups, filthy and exhausted, arriving in clumps and clusters of men, grey with dried mud and clay.

"What the heck state are you lot in? It'll be extra fatigues unless you get yourselves smartened," Michael shouted. "Bertie Middleton, when did you last have a proper shave?"

"If my razor was sharp enough to shave, it'd be all right," Bertie replied out of the corner of his mouth.

"Right, by midday tomorrow I want you all here, clean and shaved, boots and clothes scraped and brushed, rifles and bayonets cleaned." Michael raised his voice again for effect. "Is that clear?"

"Yes, sir," came the collective mumbled response.

It started with a strafing of shrapnel.

"Get your heads down!" Michael shouted.

"That's rifle grenades and 'sausages'. Shite!" Ben cursed as a canister known as a sausage landed close to their bay, showering them in sand from the split bags.

The sudden clamour was so loud they ducked and swore. Never had they experienced such close shelling. There followed two or three seconds of profound silence before screams and cries issued from all around.

"I've got sand in places that 'ave never seen the light of day," Ben said.

"I can't 'ear nothing," Bertie said, shaking his head. "Oh, Christ, the dug-out's hit. Oh, my Lord, the sergeant's got it."

"Emergency dressing! Stretcher bearer!" The cry went out.

"Oh no, Christ Almighty!" John shrank onto his haunches.

"'Old tight lad," Bertie said to John. "You've gone right pale, steady."

None of them had ever seen the inside of a man's back.

"We've had shrapnel whizzing past and shells from our own lot shrieking high over, but nothing like that," someone muttered.

The men were much quieter for the rest of the day. The enthusiasm for glory dulled.

February 1916

Dear Rose,

How ignorant we were. We thought we were so clever. We've been on the move such a lot, but we marched into this village to join the hardened troops at last. So full of optimism were we. Despite minor incidents and losing one or two brave fellows, we are, at last, nearing the thick of it.

Stupidly we marched in broad daylight with bands playing and officers astride horses. Jerry let us have it and one Captain was thrown clean across the road. I won't go into too much detail, Rose, but suffice it to say that we were lucky so many of the shells were duds. There could have been carnage. We are still amateurs at this but learning fast.

One youngster is doing a field punishment No.1 for falling out of the march in without permission. Now he is tied by his wrists to the wheel of a travelling field kitchen with his arms outstretched. He is crying and his nose is running. Rose, it is like a crucifixion. It's so horrible. He argued with the CO, which didn't help his cause. I said I needed to discipline my men, but I can't accept this is a positive image for them. It generates fear, not respect.

Perhaps I should not be telling you these things. If you would rather I didn't, please say. It helps me to unburden my thoughts, and I sense you have the strength to understand, Rose. I cannot write thus to my mother.

In the main I am doing my brave duty for King and Country and other times are quiet and dull.

When next you write, tell me of the countryside around our home with your artist's eye. Describe the scents and sounds in the lane. Let me know of your work at Lady Margaret's and tell me what interests you, dear Rose. Everything is brown and grey here. Your letters cheer me and let me know all is well in the world somewhere.

Your friend,
Michael

March 1916
Dear Michael,

I was so pleased to receive your letter, but I hope sincerely that you take no unnecessary risk whilst doing your duty, of which you can be very proud. Please tell me the truth of what you are doing, though, and how you feel. I am not your mother who needs protecting from truths, nor your sweetheart for whom you need to sound brave and courageous. I am your good friend and I have strength to help you shoulder whatever this war sends you.

I have included this tiny talisman. He is a 'Fumsup Touch Wud'. As you see, his little arms raise to touch his wooden head. If you look closely, he has a four-leaf clover on his forehead and the words 'Touch Wud' on the back of his head. The wings on his ankles are to speed you home with safety. He is yours for the duration.

The weather here is cold and grey, but I wrapped up and walked along the lane to the little shop for Mama. The fields are many shades of brown with just one here and there full of tiny green shoots of promise. I imagine it is winter wheat or barley, but it heralds the spring which surely will come.

I heard an owl last night. It was a female calling, as it seemed to say t-wit and not t-woo. It kept me awake for a while and I lay wondering *about you and what you are doing. Do you ever hear a bird sing in your grey landscape?*

I am sure you want to know that Delphi is well and so is Izzy. Our life has not changed significantly. We sew and knit for our boys abroad. Delphi is involved in a local group who bake each week and the proceeds of their labours are sent to France, to our own Manchester lads. Perhaps you will receive a box from them soon.

Keep safe, Michael. God bless you and your chums.

Your good friend,

Rose

CHAPTER 11

There was a week to go before the Easter break for the students at Lady Margaret Hall. Rose opened the telegram she received just after breakfast with trepidation. Her hands shook.

No good news ever arrived this way these days. She gasped when she read it and rushed to Miss Jex-Blake's office.

"I am so sorry to ask, but I need to go home early," Rose said, showing the Principal the telegram she had received.

"It must be serious if *you* are asking such a thing. What is the matter, my dear?"

"It's my brother. He was seventeen only last week and he's disappeared. My mother is in a terrible state and Papa has asked if I might return home."

Miss Jex-Blake stood. "We have just a week to go, and as I said it must be important for you to ask. Yes, go, Rose, and God speed. I hope the situation resolves itself."

Rose needed to explain. "My brother did this once before, in 1914. He is too young to go to war, and back then Papa proved his age and found him. He is still too young, so I hope we have the same positive ending to this sorry tale."

"Indeed. My good wishes to your parents, Rose, dear, and return to us with better news. See the porter to arrange your transport."

It took Rose two more days to arrive at her home to find her mother had retired to her bed, her sisters were in a state of shock and disarray and Dora was struggling to maintain normality.

"Oh, Miss Rose, I am so pleased to see you," Dora said. "Mrs Strong is in her room and your sisters are in the house too."

Rose sped up the stairs.

"Your father went to work today. He cannot take more time away," Mrs Strong said upon Rose's arrival.

"What has happened?"

"Hector probably travelled to Manchester. The old porter at the station remembers seeing him, and the lady in the office said that he bought a one-way ticket." With the last three words, she dissolved into tears. Her blotched face revealed she had already spent several hours crying.

"Did nobody contact you? Surely they must realise that type of ticket was not normal."

"Your Papa took his papers from last time and asked around everywhere he could think of. He has written many letters, too, but there is no trace of Hector anywhere. He has vanished." Large tears rolled down her cheeks.

"Oh, Mama, please don't be distressed. Why don't you get dressed and come downstairs with me? We shall make you comfortable on the chaise longue in the parlour by the fire, and you can take comfort in being the centre of the family again. We need you."

"It's so good to see you home, Rose. You are a real comfort."

A week passed, then ten days and still there was no news.

"The last person I saw suggested he has joined up under a false name so he cannot be traced," Mr Strong said at breakfast one morning. "Apparently it's common among those too young."

Mrs Strong wailed. "We may never find him!"

"Mama, take comfort from the fact he is doing what he most desires. I'm sure there will be news and we shall rejoice again," Rose said. "We must be proud of his strength and determination to serve his King and Country."

Delphi sighed and Izzy left her chair to put her arms around her mother.

That evening, Rose wrote to Michael.

April 1916
My dear Michael,

Things here are not happy. Hector has absconded again. This time I believe we will not find him. We think he has changed his name so he could join a regiment and go abroad to fight, even though he is nowhere near old enough. I am sure you can imagine how distraught Mama has become, and it is quiet and solemn here.

The wasted woodlands and skeletal trees have cried their leaves, and I am sad too. There is a crystal nip to the air here, and I fear we may be in for more bad weather before the winter is done even though spring should be arriving. Enough! I'm sorry for being gloomy. In the meantime, I am pleased the rain has eased and I hope it has for you. The sun pierced the clouds today. The rays shone down on us like a blessing and the robin visited the kitchen garden as Mr Yates dug carrots for our dinner. It sang as I went out to pick herbs for Dora. I needed the fresh air.

I am knitting socks as fast as I am able. I understand from the newspaper this is one small way we at home can assist our brave soldiers. Delphi is still doing much voluntary work. I'm sure she thinks of you often and misses you too.

I wonder how you are daily. Please keep safe and in good spirits.
Your good friend,
Rose

Michael was heading for a new destination as Rose wrote. He was on the move yet again nearer to the front. He arrived on the banks of the Somme after a strenuous march through rain-soaked countryside.

"I'm drenched through to me bones," Bertie said to him as they came to a village. "It's so bitter I'm tensed against it all the time. It's not normal to be so soaked. I can't even smoke. Me cigs are saturated too."

"We're here now. Bray is a small place, but there should be somewhere for a bath and bed if we are lucky," Michael responded.

"It's more than a bath I need. I've got enough lice to supply the 'ole of the region. I can't sleep at night for the itching," Bertie said.

"We'll take ourselves to the medic and get that Blue Unction. That should 'elp for a short while." Ben scratched as he spoke.

"I think I'm in Hell here," John said.

"Not yet, yer not, me boy," came a response. "You wait, mate."

"That's enough," Michael said, putting a stop to the conversation before it got too depressing. "Back into trenches soon and then we'll be going forward and scouting properly, not just practising. You'll enjoy that, boys." Michael tried to sound positive, but in truth he was so tired and wet himself he wanted to drop in the nearest doorway and sleep for a year.

The next night, Michael wrote to his parents and to Rose.

April 1916
My dear Rose,

There is a masochistic alignment in this harsh challenge and different circumstances in which I find myself. We are back in the trench too quickly, but I have a sense of positive purpose.

There has been so much rain and snow over the last few weeks this place is awash and it's impossible to keep dry. We hacked off the bottoms of our greatcoats after a fellow got lodged in the mud. We all had to heave him out and he lost his boots.

The smell is the worst. Perhaps I should not tell you this. I am concerned for your female sensibility, but I sense you have the strength to let me share things with you. I suggest that Delphi would be mortified, and Izzy is yet too young and fragile. Dearest Rose, forgive me but the old mud in which men have lived for months without sanitation is pungent to say the least. Scraps of food attract rats which drown, and their decay added to the waste and excrement of so many humans is an assault on the senses. We must learn to ignore it. Some wag came up with an idea. His attempt to mask this enduring unpleasantness is to burn incense from the church in our brazier. It is a subject of hot debate whether it's an improvement.

I shall finish this later, Rose, as I must go out and do my scouting now. I shall return in several hours.

Well, here I am again. I have been out listening and observing. The most difficult part is lying still for so long, but I was lucky on this occasion. There was a dip in the land where rubbish had been left some time ago, but I could lie along the length of the midden and be hidden from the Hun.

One fellow, Billy Masters, was not so lucky, though. He acquired a pair of binoculars from a chap in the village where we are billeted. We discussed who should have them, but the consensus was that he who found them could use them. He got them out as we lay hidden, and I was in the middle of saying 'watch how you use those, mate,' when there was a bang and he was gone. A sniper caught the glint and got him as quick as a blink. He just slid slowly and rolled over and that was that. I don't think he felt anything, so accurate are those crack shots. We waited until dark and slithered back here to the safety of the trench.

I have your Fumsup to keep me company. When I am lonely, I rub his little head with my thumb and raise his arms to touch the wood to be safe. I'm sure the wings on his ankles will bring me quickly home in the end.

It's so bleak and raw tonight the ground is hardening, which is a blessing. I'm in my dugout now so that's not so bad, but when we are back lying outside for hours on end it's more difficult. We wriggle our fingers and toes without being seen.

Thank you for listening to my chatter, Rose. It is a great release for me. God keep you well. I look forward to your socks.

I am thankful to call myself your friend,
Michael

CHAPTER 12

"A new fellow joins us tomorrow." Michael gave the morning briefing before breakfast and rifle cleaning. "He's an Australian, but he joined up in Scotland where he's been preaching."

"Gawd 'elp us," said Bertie. "A Bible-basher. Is he coming as a padre, then?"

"No, he signed up as a private, and now he's got a promotion like me so he's a lieutenant. He's to replace Billy Masters, so he's a ground scout too. He did his training on Salisbury Plain as we all did."

"What's 'is name then, this Aussie?"

"George Dight. Lieutenant George Dight."

"'E doesn't sound like one of us, does 'e, wiv a name like that?" Bertie looked sideways and nudged Ben.

After breakfast, Michael met George.

"Welcome to the 19th Manchesters." Michael extended his hand to the newcomer and looked up into a large, open, freckled face with light brown eyes. George had short red hair with a curl that struggled to escape from his officer's cap. He was half a head taller and broader than Michael, and wore a moustache.

"Thank you. My passage through training got delayed because I had intended to sign up as a padre, but it took so long I opted to join the Royal Scots as a private. I wanted to get on with it. The delays were so frustrating. Anyhow, now I'm here attached to your lot."

His broad Australian accent sounded alien to Michael.

"I was called to Edinburgh Castle for training," George continued. "I was a Grammar School boy and graduated in arts at the University of Sydney, so promotions came along, and then I had the opportunity to do the ground scout training."

Michael nodded. "Come and meet some of the men. Others are in the village making the most of their time here. There are still several local French families and French troops, of course. We're six miles from the fire trench, so we're able to have proper rest. There isn't much here, but it's comparatively safe at the moment. We'll be heading back into the trenches soon enough, so it's good for us all to unwind and relax. We've not had much serious stuff, but we've lost a few good souls."

"How's the grub?"

"Grub?"

"Rations, mate, how's the rations?"

"Oh, right. They vary a lot. Sometimes we get bacon and beans, but more and more it's good old bully beef. The lads are trading cigarettes and tobacco from home for French bread. That's very good," Michael explained. "The corned beef is so salty we can't always eat it, so we've buried the tins to make a firmer foundation on which to walk. It's been so muddy and wet here."

"And the men, what are they like? Any old bludgers I should know?"

"Bludger? What's that?"

"Oh, sorry mate. A bludger's a lazy bloke." George asked his questions with a sparkle about him to which Michael warmed. His face, freckled and round, was without guile.

"They're a good bunch, in the main; a mixed lot. We're from the same area originally. They're wondering about you too. They know you preached in Scotland."

"Oh, bloody hell." George laughed and his eyes shone. "I might have views on the Almighty, but they're mine and I'll not be preaching them here. I like a drink as much as the next man, too."

"Do you fancy heading to the local estaminet for a bite to eat?"

"That would be good, mate. Thanks."

"It's basic, but the food isn't bad and makes a change from Fray Bentos. There're a couple of mademoiselles pleasing to the eye. Their father keeps a strict watch on them, but it's fun to have a go even if it will get us nowhere. There are others, of course."

"I'm happy to give the molls a miss. I've no intention of getting a dose." George grimaced and then laughed.

"Me neither," agreed Michael. *He must be older than me if he's been through university, but I'm going to like this man*, he thought.

Michael and George strolled together into the centre of the village. The sun was going down and the sky was shades of pearl. The air was crisp and clean and fresh.

"This is easy on the soul," George said, nodding towards the sky and the setting sun. "What has the action been like lately?"

Michael gave a brief account of recent observations made of their Jerry opponents, and then they shared information about themselves.

"Have you got a girl back home?" George asked.

"No," Michael answered. "There is a family, though, with three daughters. One is too young. The middle girl is a beauty but immature and too forthright for me. The oldest, Rose, is interesting. She's clever and concerned and thoughtful."

"Sounds like you're interested in her," George said with a grin.

"Oh, no, it's not that. We're just friends."

As they chatted, another young man headed to the same eating place from the opposite direction.

Several individuals and groups of men walked with shoulders hunched against the cold. The lone man was shorter than the rest, but he was broad. His collar was up and a long woollen scarf protected his nose and mouth as well as the top of his head, so that only his eyes showed. A solitary figure, he walked with purpose.

The shutters of the small houses had been closed early against the bitter chill. Little slits of light could be seen here and there. Where an occasional glimmer shone unhindered, tables covered in oilcloths and with families huddled around could be spotted. Sounds of animals were heard as they stomped in stables or little barns attached to the living accommodation, which added to the homely atmosphere. It was a false calm. The men knew what horrors lay within a stone's throw.

As they walked through the village, aromas made their mouths salivate. Garlic and hot goose fat, bread and other smells they did not recognise. Michael and George walked more quickly in anticipation of a fried egg and good salty chips with a large hunk of fresh bread.

"These houses are almost unscathed," George noted.

"This place has been lucky so far. Keep your fingers crossed that Jerry lets us eat before he tries it."

As they got to the door, a small queue stamped and rubbed their hands to force out the cold. Once inside, they were greeted by the sound of men enjoying the relaxed atmosphere. No particular conversation could be heard, but now and then a guffaw rose above the hubbub.

"That one's Mathilde." Michael nodded towards a young woman. "She's adept at avoiding straying hands. You watch. Her sister's over there."

"Long hours of practice by the look of it," George said and smiled, showing strong white teeth below his officer's moustache.

A few feet in front of them stood the young man of stocky build. At that moment, he turned and pushed his scarf back from his face as he approached the head of the queue.

"My God, Hector!" Michael gasped and called out. "Hector, over here! It's Michael Redfern."

The man looked at the door and shrugged. Relinquishing his place, he jostled his way through the close throng a few places back.

"I can't believe it. Rose wrote and told me they thought you had come over here. What are the chances of us meeting up like this? What are you doing here?"

"It's not that much of a coincidence," Hector answered. "All the Manchesters are in this area."

"George, this is the brother of those sisters back at home I told you about," Michael explained. "Hector, you're seventeen. Your family are so worried."

"You must understand, Michael. This is something I needed to do, and I'm not Hector Strong here," he said in an undertone, glancing sideways. "My name is Harry Stone."

"How did you get away with it?"

"They don't demand any real form of identity and certainly no proof of age," he replied.

"That's true," George added. "Even for me, a foreigner with my accent, although we're in the Commonwealth. There wasn't much formal checking. They took my word for it."

They stood to one side as a large group of men passed, having finished their meal.

"Here we go," Michael said. "Come on, Hec— Harry, and you can tell us your full story."

Coffee circles stained the oilcloth, but as they sat on old wooden chairs at the table one of the girls scurried over and wiped it with a grey cloth. The men didn't mind.

"*Messieurs.*" She nodded at them and smiled. "*Omelettes et frites?*"

George rubbed his hands in anticipation rather than cold now. "*Oui, oui, s'il vous plâit. Et trois bières.*"

"I could eat a horse and chase its rider," Hector said.

"So, where've you been and what have you been doing?" asked Michael.

The girl brought three glasses and plonked a jug of pale beer on the table. Next, a basket with chunks of crusty bread arrived. The three men dived on the food.

"Well, obviously, I gave a false name," said Hector. "They weren't bothered at the recruitment. I'd worked out an age and date of birth beforehand. I passed the medical."

"That wasn't much either!"

"No. They sent me to Aldershot for training, and when they wanted volunteers as runners, I put up my hand. Then we came over here. We did final training at a place outside Boulogne."

"So, are you saying you're a runner?" George asked.

"That's right," Hector answered.

George and Michael exchanged a quick glance.

Trench warfare necessitated lots of runners. It was the most efficient method of passing messages between the trenches and to Headquarters, but it was also extremely dangerous. Often the messenger would climb up to ground level and run towards the other trench to find the quickest and least congested route. While up on the ground, the soldier became exposed to enemy lookouts. It was common for runners to die before reaching their destination. Usually runners were young. Michael had three to take his observations back to the Headquarters' dugout.

"We had a baptism of fire during the first day in the reserve line. One platoon of 'A' Company was almost wiped out during rifle inspection and I helped to carry a fellow, one of our first dead, to the dressing station. That night we counted our casualties. We tried to estimate how long our life would last by dividing the number of dead and wounded into the strength of the battalion." The two older men watched his face as he spoke. "We weren't in a spirit of despair, but we wanted to face the facts and work out our percentage chance of making it through. I know as a runner I might not see the end, but it's marvellous fun and the thrill I get from a successful run is fantastic. It's a great wheeze, all this."

Hector shifted in his chair and heaved his coat off his shoulders as he chewed on the bread. Neither George nor Michael knew what to say to this speech of realism from one so young.

"I had a letter from Rose," Michael announced into the silence. "She said how they worried but she did write she was proud that you are doing what you most want."

Their omelettes and chips arrived. No traditional horse fat could be found these days. All the animals not in use were too old and stringy even for the knacker's knife, so the chips were cooked in goose fat.

Silence descended again as the three men ate with pleasure. Each took small forkfuls to make the experience last as long as possible; not only for the food, but also for the sweaty, steamy warmth of the place.

"Are you going to write home? It would put their minds at ease. You don't need to give any information other than that you're all right," Michael said.

"I suppose I should." As they finished eating, Hector put his hands over his stomach and sighed. "It's Rose I miss most. She always understands. She doesn't need to gush, but she gets to the nub of the issue."

Michael was aware of George's glance towards him, but he was in a faraway place with a slight crease to his forehead.

CHAPTER 13

Rose received a short note from her brother. At least it reassured her he was alive and in good health. Hector had not written to either parent, and Rose had to break the news to them. That evening she took a deep breath and held the envelope towards her father.

"Papa, I have news for you and Mama. It's not bad," she added swiftly as dread flitted across his face. She sat opposite him and waited while he extracted the note. He looked at the signature and glanced up at her before reading the contents with care.

April 1916
Dearest Rose,

I met Michael Redfern and his friend George. They said I should write to allay fears. I dare not write to Papa or Mama. I really do not want to be found. I suppose they will be distressed and for that I am sorry. I daresay this is cowardly of me, but I'm happy here and proud to be doing my bit.

I write to you to explain, because I know you will not judge me as harshly as our parents. This is something I must do, and Papa would not allow it. I was shocked at first by the amount I have to carry. I thought I was a pack mule rather than a soldier, but the job I have here now means less weight to heave along. I am fulfilling my destiny. I am respected for what I do.

Please give my fondest love to the family.
Your dear brother,
Hector

P.S. Michael asked me to send his good wishes and says he often thinks of you and what you might be doing. The chap he was with is from Australia. We had a good meal and exchanged news. The other fellow called it a 'yabber', but he meant a talk.

H.

"I don't understand why he wrote to me alone," Rose said with a frown. "He writes of being cowardly in this, but clearly he is not. Maybe he feels shame because of the way that he left. He seems to think he had no choice but that." Rose tried to soften the blow. "I thought it best to show it to you first. Mama and the girls know nothing of this."

"Well done, Rose. That was a wise decision. I shall take it and share it with Mama now. Please do not say anything to Delphi or Izzy yet. Perhaps you would join me."

"Of course, Papa."

They took the letter to Mrs Strong.

"I can't believe that is all he says. And why did he not write to me?" Mrs Strong showed her dismay and a tinge of anger radiated across the room towards her hapless husband. "I don't understand why they allow boys to be there."

"My dear, we must remain calm since we cannot alter the circumstances. Pray he remains safe and that he is brought back to us. He says he is happy and well."

"He shouldn't be fighting at all. Hector is just a boy. Can they not see that? Surely they know he is not old enough. And what job is he doing that means he has less kit to carry? Do you think he is in an office and away from the action, then?"

Later, Rose wandered through the house in a restless mood. *So Hector has met Michael and says he thinks of me. I wonder if it is as often as Hector suggests?*

Rose, her mother and two sisters were in town the next day for a meeting of the local 'Workers for Soldiers' group. The agenda this time was rolling bandages rather than packing boxes of treats or knitting.

"Mrs Blount has asked me to make some posters," Rose informed them. "I had a letter from her yesterday. She wants to ask for donations of soap, toothbrushes, notepads and pencils. I understand the posters will be placed in local shop windows. It's a small service that most people will achieve."

"That should be a task that suits your artistic talents well, my dear," Mrs Strong said.

"Lucky you," Delphi remarked sourly. "That sounds much more fun than rolling bandages."

"We've got a good lot of socks and balaclava helmets here. At least the group will know we are not slacking at home." Izzy indicated the bag that Mrs Strong held.

As they walked towards the hall where the meeting was to take place, Rose caught sight of a familiar figure limping across the road towards them. His stick tapped to the uneven rhythm of his steps.

"Good day, ladies." Thom touched his hat as he greeted them. "Are you shopping on this fair day?"

"We are going to a meeting at the Salvation Army hall to support our boys at the front," Delphi said.

Thom pulled a wry face. "Everyone is doing something to help. Prime Minister Asquith's Military Service Bill will become law soon, I am sure. Conscription will help to fill the declining numbers who are enlisting. I am unfit to fight abroad because of this blasted leg and my lungs being so feeble, so I registered my interest in war work in Manchester at the barrack's offices. It's a likely scenario for me. At least I shall be in a uniform and doing my bit too."

"I'm sure you will accomplish whatever you are able, Thom." Rose smiled at him.

"May I accompany you ladies to the door of your meeting?"

"Why, thank you, Thom. That is most gentlemanly of you," Mrs Strong said.

Izzy and Delphi flanked their mother and they proceeded in front. Thom took his place on the edge of the pavement next to Rose.

Rose knew Thom had tried to enlist with the others, but his childhood disability had prevented him from joining a fighting force. She had not questioned him about it before, but now he had brought it up she asked, "When did your problem start?"

"I developed scoliosis in early childhood. It's a spinal problem. Often it can correct itself to a large degree with minimal help. Sadly, I am one of the ten per cent upon whom it has caused deformity. I'm a poor specimen, Rose."

"And I am as blind as a mole without my glasses. What a pair we are."

"A pair, indeed," Thom said with undisguised feeling. "I'm unsure if I shall live in the barracks and whether training will take me elsewhere. Before I leave, I would like to take you out to dinner one evening; somewhere special. I know you came home from your college early at Easter, but when do you return?"

"I shan't be returning. There is far too much going on, and Mama needs me at home."

"That seems sad," Thom said.

"I am disappointed, but it's my duty to be here and I've been so very lucky for the experience."

Thom called to collect Rose the following week. He had booked a table at the very smart hotel on the edge of town. It had been built during the Victorian era and had magnificent Gothic architecture. She felt special when he handed her down from the carriage and swept her in through the wide front door held open for them by an elderly footman. The waiter held her chair and once seated he spread her serviette for her with a flourish.

"We are fortunate in England that we have no food rationing. From what I read the Russians, in particular, are in a bad way with many of the ordinary people starving. I don't think German families are doing well either," Rose said.

"Perhaps they should have thought of that before starting all this. I'm not sure if we will hold out here if this war keeps going. I'm sure the government will need to implement some sort of control."

"You may be correct. In the meantime, this is wonderful. I do feel somewhat guilty, though. I know our boys over there are not always eating well." Rose looked about her.

They were seated at a table with a thick white cloth. The silver shone and the candles sparkled on the glassware.

"How have you heard that?"

"I have letters from time to time from Michael."

"Oh, I see." Thom looked at his hands in his lap.

"I think to write to me is a release. He tells me things he might not wish to tell his mother. It's just as a friend," Rose clarified. "He writes to Delphi too, although she doesn't share her news much. It must be too personal."

"Ah." Thom smiled at her. "I'm sure you are a good and reliable friend, Rose, but I hope you might consider me as a good friend or even more."

Rose, unsure how to respond, smiled back and nodded vaguely.

"I hope you don't mind being seen out with a hobbling fellow."

"Oh, Thom, of course not. You are a dear friend."

Rose had much to consider following her outing. It was late by the time the taxicab dropped her home and she thanked Thom sincerely. He took her hand in both of his when she offered it for him to shake. She had enjoyed her evening immensely.

He is a kind and gentle man. Life has not been easy for him with his disability, she thought. *He hasn't received a white feather of cowardice, thankfully. The women who give those out are cruel. I suppose his condition is obvious. I know he feels their stares, though.*

"Have you had a good time?" Izzy was already in bed when Rose entered their shared bedroom. "Does this mean you have a beau? Will you marry him?" Izzy was as romantic and innocent as ever.

"Hush, Izzy. Go to sleep."

Rose lay awake for a long time. Izzy's words echoed around her head. She knew with certainty that Thom had strong feelings for her. This outing had taken their friendship to another level. They had known each other quite a while now. If she could not be with Michael, perhaps she should reconcile her mind and her heart to taking someone else. She might even grow to love him, in a way.

Perhaps that is enough. I should not be desperate for a shattering, soaring romance. Who am I to be so greedy?

CHAPTER 14

The next morning, two letters lay on the salver on the hall table. Rose yawned and covered her mouth as she descended the stairs, unaware that one awaited her. Despite her newfound resolve, her heart let her down as soon as she saw the now familiar writing. It jumped in her chest until she was winded. She realised the same hand heralded Delphi's attendance and knew a moment of jealousy. She couldn't help but feel anticipation of her own correspondence as she carefully used the little knife that lay beside the plate to slit the seal.

May 1916

My dear Rose,

A new month but it's the same routine. I crawled across No Man's Land during the early hours and lay as still as death, (pardon the pun). I could hear the enemy in their trenches and listened to their coughing and whispers and snoring as if they were in the next room. It was so desperately cold. I was very grateful for your gloves and muffler, dear Rose. What a friend you are. There is none better. I was only supposed to be there for two hours, but it turned out to be much, much longer. This cold weather should be long past but still it lingers.

We lost several good chaps over the last few days to a sniper. We could not understand how they could see our boys even down in the trench, which is on higher ground than theirs. I listened and watched and eventually spotted a false tree on the edge of the wood. Yes, that's right, it was a mock-up with a ladder against it and Jerry was up there. I sent my runner with the information and that was the end of their little game.

Rose took a breath and tried to still her shaking fingers.

There is a chance that I may get some leave soon. It will be only for three or four days and by the time I have travelled my time will be short at home, but it'll be worth it.

I have made a good friend here and shall bring him with me. His name is George Dight. He is older than me by five years but is a really good chap. I'm not sure what I would do without him now. We are companions in mirth, in dread, in fear and in the work that we do here as the eyes and ears of the company.

I hope we may meet when I am on leave. Perhaps you and Delphi might come to the store and we could all share an afternoon tea.

This is the nub of the matter. He wishes to see Delphi again, Rose thought. All her emotions were on a fairground swing-boat. One minute her heart was in her mouth and the next it was through the floor.

I shall let you know when I return as soon as I know myself, dear Rose.

Rose paused again. *Oh, why does he call me that?*

I look forward to your next letter. In the meantime, I send my fond good wishes.
Your very good friend,
Michael

Rose folded the letter carefully and put it in her pocket as she moved towards the dining room.

As Rose wound honey around her spoon ready to drizzle it on her porridge, Delphi swept into the room with a spring in her step. She twirled and her hair swung out around her in a dark cloud.

"Do you like my new shawl? It's so soft and I just adore the colour."

"That shade of lilac suits you well," Rose responded. "Papa is very generous."

"He knows I didn't have the opportunity that you had, going to college and all the money involved. He understands I have needs too."

"Of course," Rose agreed with mildness. "Have you heard from Michael?" She enquired with a casualness she did not feel. Since she'd found her letter first, her sister had no knowledge of it.

"Yes, I have, as a matter of fact."

"What did he have to say?" Rose turned away from her towards the table. She didn't want Delphi to see her anxiety.

"I shan't read all of it."

She's trying to be enigmatic, Rose thought.

"Some of it is very private, as you can imagine," Delphi added more candidly. "I know he loves me. Surely when he returns on leave, he will realise that we cannot wait for this stupid war to end." A smile tickled her face. She took the letter from its little envelope and read aloud, "*It seems that I may get some home leave for some extra specialist training. It will be only for three or four days. I think we may be having a Big Push soon.*

"*I have made a good friend here and shall bring him with me. His name is George Dight. I think you will like him. He is from Australia and so cannot return to visit his family.*

"He goes on to say how much he is looking forward to seeing me again," she said, avoiding Rose's gaze. "Anyway, when are you meeting Thom again?"

"We are going for a walk this afternoon in the park if it stays dry."

"He seems very keen," Delphi said. "You suit each other. He's a bit dull for me, though." She was unaware of the insult she had just delivered.

"He has many sterling qualities that are not evident immediately. You need to get to know him better, Delphi, and you would see. Don't always be influenced by what you perceive on the surface. That's very shallow."

"Huh! Listen to you, Missy Know-all."

"Girls, what is it now?" Mrs Strong entered the room.

"Nothing at all, Mama," Rose said. "How are you feeling this morning?"

"I slept a little better. Is that a letter, Delphi?"

"It's from Michael Redfern. He thinks he may have a few days at home before some 'Big Push', whatever that means."

"He might have further news of Hector." Tears came to Mrs Strong's eyes, even after all this time. "When is he coming? Do you think he will know something?"

"We don't know exactly when Michael will be here, Mama," Rose said, getting up and putting her cheek to that of her mother. "Please remember that Hector is pursuing what he loves, and we must be proud of what he is doing."

Some days later, Rose and Thom strolled in the park again. The smell of the damp garden full of rose bushes waiting to bloom with lavender around their borders was intoxicating.

"I know nothing of the roses' names, but they are a beautiful sign that spring will return," Rose said.

Thom bent and plucked a wisp of lavender and presented it to her. "Beautiful indeed," he said, and her cheeks grew warm.

"Thank you," she managed.

As they sauntered further, Rose said, "It seems as if there is something planned to take place in France soon. The papers are full of the extra men being sent and munitions that are gathering over there. It is no secret." She twirled the lavender under her nose abstractedly.

"I read these things too," Thom answered. "Vast preparations are taking place behind the lines, apparently. It's all happening between Albert and Amiens. Isn't Michael around there somewhere? There is increased raiding activity, and the registration of artillery clearly demonstrates an attack is imminent. The allied press is full of a coming 'Big Push'. I cannot see the wisdom of informing the enemy."

"It does seem reckless. I suppose there must be some particular thinking behind all the talk, but I would have thought it better to make it a surprise." Rose was unsure exactly where Michael was but at the mention of his name, she felt a little breathless.

"It seems the only surprise will be the exact date and time, although the way things are sounding this'll be announced too, for all to hear," Thom said.

He said he would be home on leave before this Big Push. If only he could be here when it occurs. He would miss it and be safe, Rose thought. She glanced sideways at Thom, who fortunately seemed not to notice that she had gone quiet. "Shall we sit for a moment?" She moved towards a bench without waiting for his response, feeling traitorous and uneasy.

She liked Thom's company, but her deepest thoughts were miles away across the sea. Here she was enjoying white clouds and mild sunshine with the clean perfume of lavender. The grass was a hundred delicate shades of green and subtle pink shoots dotted the rose bush stems. Those overseas were seeing only grey and brown with broken stumps of trees and the bitter odour of desolation. She remembered Michael's description of the trench smells. How did he bear it? He was as sensitive as anyone.

Oh Michael, why cannot I be content that I have Thom as a suitor and be happy for my sister? She is careless of your attention. She takes it for granted. She does not write to you often, I know. Why are you on my mind so regularly when it is not me you desire?

"Are you all right, Rose, my dear? You seem distracted today."

"Oh, Thom, I'm sorry. Yes, I'm well. It's just this awful war. It seems to be never-ending, and all our brave boys are suffering." *I should have known he would indeed notice my silences. He is always perceptive. Dear Thom.*

"Not all," Thom said, looking glum. "I'm in uniform now but only travelling to Manchester and back. It's not exactly heroic."

"That is not your fault. You have suffered in the past in ways beyond the understanding of most of us. I know your work is secret; therefore it must be valuable for those out there and requires your sharp brain. Not everyone could do what you do." She placed her hand on his arm and smiled up at him with genuine warmth. She stood. "Come, let's stroll some more and take pleasure in this day as best we might. All of you are serving the war effort so that such as I can be free. I will not betray that by refusing to enjoy the sun."

Or feeling sorry for myself and wondering how Michael is over there, she thought to herself.

CHAPTER 15

The atmosphere seemed to crackle with anticipation. Michael was home. Rose would meet him this afternoon with Delphi. The invitation had finally arrived yesterday. She knew in her heart it was her lovely sister he wanted to greet, but she would be relieved to receive proof he was not shattered in mind or body. In Manchester, young men could be seen hobbling or bandaged, having been injured during their time abroad. But now that Michael was back, Rose bubbled with barely concealed joy and excitement.

"Good morning, Delphi, dear," she grinned as her sister entered the dining room. "What a beautiful day. It will be chilly with this stiff breeze, but the sun is so bright, and the dew is like diamonds hanging from the rose bushes out there. See? Just look!"

"Yes, it's delightful," Delphi answered but hardly turned her slender neck to observe.

"You must be so excited to be seeing Michael again. It has been such a long time for you." Rose could not resist prodding this thought which was like a wound for her.

"Mmm, yes, of course," Delphi said, but she was unusually self-contained on this intoxicating day.

A puzzled frown creased Rose's forehead. "I suppose it is nerve-racking to meet again after such a time apart and with so much happening. It is normal, I'm sure, to suffer so."

Delphi sighed. "I don't think you have any comprehension of how I suffer, Rose," she said with uncharacteristic wistful quietude.

The surprising tenor to Delphi's mercurial temperament caught Rose unawares. She had anticipated a loud rebuke for her comment, not this thoughtful reticence. Was Delphi growing up at last? She had shown no other signs and seldom wrote to Michael during his long absence. When she did, it was because Rose encouraged her, and she dashed off a note with haste. However, it was only recently that Delphi had reminded her older sister of his letters to her, including personal messages of a romantic nature. She had left Rose in no doubt as to his feelings for her.

He must be particularly sweet on her to put up with her appearance of carelessness, Rose thought.

The morning crept along for her. She attended to her sewing and mending while Izzy had her music lesson and Delphi shut herself away somewhere, saying she was going to read. Rose drew from her deep well of determination to complete her tasks. The temptation to wander around and do little was almost overwhelming. Mr Strong came home for lunch as usual and the conversation, for once, was desultory. He tried to engage his girls in talk of the latest events. There was little of major import to discuss other than the grinding news from across the Channel, and Mrs Strong had been sensitive to any debate of this nature since Hector's departure.

After an interminable hour, it was time for the two older Strong sisters to put on their afternoon finery and catch the motor omnibus.

"You seem more jaunty this afternoon," Rose observed as her sister twisted back and forth in an attempt to survey the bow at the back of her dress.

"Is this tied prettily enough? I really can't see," Delphi said. "I so detest a ribbon that is not straight and fettled properly."

"Let me just straighten this part," Rose said as she unfurled the fabric on one of the loops.

Delphi spun for her sister's approval. Then she faced Rose, patting her hair and curling a tendril around her finger.

She knows how fetching she looks, Rose thought. *Perhaps she has overcome her nerves and is now excited again.*

They entered Redfern's Department Store together and made their way to the tearoom.

"I feel slightly nervous," Rose admitted, "even if you don't."

"Oh Rose, don't be soft."

Delphi tossed her head. The delicate feathers on her hat floated and the tendrils of hair waved prettily. Her smile was fixed, and Rose caught a glimpse of how she really felt. As they entered Summer Court, under the archway, murmurs of conversation assailed them, and good quality china clinked as people enjoyed a refined afternoon tea. Rose scanned the crowded space. A lady laughed a little too loudly and heads turned. A whiskered gentleman stood to help his companion from her chair. Delphi stood on her toes to get a better view. They hesitated as they looked around for Michael and his friend.

"I hope we are not early," Delphi said with a charming little frown. "That would be bad form. We don't want to appear eager."

"Over there." Rose nudged her sister's arm and nodded across the room.

At the same time Michael came towards them, and his companion stood and awaited their approach. Rose put out her hand.

"My dear friend," Michael said, clicking his heels smartly, taking her fingers and bowing slightly. Rose knew she flushed. He repeated the process with Delphi. Then he grinned mischievously at his own formality and said, "It's so good to be home, even for a short time. Come and meet the best chap in the world."

Guiding them through the throng, they arrived at the table. "This is my very best friend, George Dight."

"Ladies, g'day to you both," George said with enthusiasm and they all shook hands.

He held a chair for Delphi. Michael did the same for Rose before taking the seat beside her. He ordered tea and there was an awkward silence.

Delphi took over. "So, our brave boys, what have you been up to?" She smiled her most radiant smile and took in the whole company. "You both look so gallant in those uniforms. I'm fully certain you will defeat any fearsome enemy." She glanced sideways at George and smiled up at him through her lashes.

She is playing the company as she always does, thought Rose.

On this occasion, she was happy to let Delphi chatter on and observe the beloved face so close to her. He looked tired, and on either side of his mouth the lines were slightly deeper. His eyes were as blue as ever as they watched Delphi, but there were little crow's feet at the corners which only added to his attraction for Rose. His shoulders had broadened, and as he sat the fabric of his trousers stretched across his thighs. She felt a tingle up her spine and a swooping in her stomach. She had missed what Delphi was saying, but George's strange accent impinged on her consciousness as he answered her.

"I would have struggled a lot more if it hadn't been for this bloke here," he said. "I think we keep each other sane."

"Yes, it's mutual," Michael added, smiling. "He's a good chap, the best, even if he says weird words and other complete rubbish sometimes."

112

Their afternoon tea arrived.

"Rose, as you are the oldest you can be 'mother'," Delphi said.

Rose knew this was so that her sister could continue to flirt, which she did outrageously with George in particular. He was fresh game for her, but he seemed impervious. He laughed and joked with Michael. Rose was happy enough to have the ordered occupation of pouring the tea and all four became a relaxed and merry company.

"My goodness, sir, you are brave to have come from the other side of the world to defend us," Delphi said, looking at George with her most flirtatious eyes.

"I need to help protect the Mother Country. We from 'down under' have a great respect, loyalty and affinity. You could do the same. There are plenty of openings for young ladies. You could go nursing, drive an ambulance or work in a factory. Mind you, you'd have to forego that enchanting little hat."

Delphi looked long and hard at George. Then she tossed her pretty head and said, "You never know, I just might. I can be as hardworking as anyone if I decide to be."

"Papa would have something to say about that, Delphi," Rose reminded her sister.

Delphi ignored this.

The next hour passed in a whirl of happiness for Rose. She revelled in the company and shut out feelings of creeping anxiety for the future.

Reluctant to bring the afternoon to a close, none of them could utter those words of imminent departure.

"Perhaps we might all take a stroll through the park tomorrow," suggested Michael. "I believe it is supposed to be slightly warmer than today with some sunshine, and I would love to have those sights and sweet smells back with me."

Rose raised her eyebrows at Delphi in silent enquiry, but before there was an agreed acquiescence Delphi answered.

"That would be very agreeable, wouldn't it, Rose?" She glanced up at George and smiled dazzlingly. Rose glanced at Michael to gauge his reaction to her sister's blatant flirting. She saw his eyes lower and then rise again to gaze at Delphi, and her heart shrank as she inwardly sighed.

Arrangements were made and the girls stood to receive help with their outdoor clothing. At the doorway, Delphi turned and gave a little wave to the two men who watched them leave.

"My goodness, she's a handful, that one." George laughed and his eyes sparkled at the memory of Delphi's outrageousness. "It would be fun to tame her, though."

"She certainly is a beauty and very lively," Michael said. "More than I can handle at the moment with everything else that's going on."

"I wouldn't mind trying. Would I be stepping on your toes, mate?"

"No, absolutely not. Good luck with that, though. She may lead you a merry dance before time is up."

"Oh, I think I have her measure," George said and smiled. "She clearly needs the experience of an older man." He grinned roguishly before gazing into the distance. "I need someone like her. She would not let me take myself too seriously. If I ever get back to parish work, she would distract me from over-solemnity. Life would be exciting and exhilarating, in a good way. Not like it is over there. Not dark and grubby and bathed in fear."

Rose was irritable.

"Why did you flirt with George so scandalously? He seems very nice, and I'm sure he doesn't deserve you playing with him. What of Michael and his feelings?"

Delphi was enigmatic in her response. "Really, Rose, don't be stuffy. George is old. He can handle himself." She paused. "Mind you, he is very attractive — in an old sort of way. His face is open and honest, and it could not be said that he is good-looking in the sultry sense, but he has charm. Those light brown eyes sparkle when he smiles. Mmm, I like that." She shrugged. "It was fun. Michael is happy to be in my company. He knows where we stand."

"I saw how Michael watched you," Rose persisted. "Don't be cruel to either of them, Delphi. Not at the moment."

"George didn't respond to my teasing. He is very..." She paused. "He is very mature. That is admirable in a man."

"What you mean is, he is not taken in by your games. He has your measure," Rose said. "They face such horror and they must leave so soon."

"Rose, let us not think about that yet. We still have tomorrow."

CHAPTER 16

Delphi walked with her chin held up, proud of the look she created for this very special afternoon. Her hat framed her face and was a striking shade of peacock blue. It matched her garment beneath the coat she wore. The dress had taken nearly five yards of crêpe de Chine, and the princess style with a cinched waist, long peplum, and bishop sleeves emphasised her elegantly tall figure. She chose to wear the collar closed high rather than open, which gave her a demure look.

Delphi's last encounter with Michael at the department store before he'd left for initial training swooped into her mind. She felt breathless with resentment and anger. How could he have been so cruel? She had covered her anger and nervousness well yesterday and had been able to give her attentions to George Dight as a diversion.

I'll teach Rose to be so smug and clever all the time, she thought.

Rose had decided upon a light green and pink dress which suited her well. She looked particularly pretty today because she was very happy. Her face shone with elation and it was infectious to those around her.

Their anticipation was high as they approached the park. The gates came into view, where they'd arranged to meet Michael and George.

"They are there," Delphi said. "George looks very fine, does he not? Not in a handsome way like Michael but in a distinguished stately way. He has a prominent air. I think he would be noticeable in a crowd."

Rose looked at her sister with fresh perspective but said nothing.

"Thank goodness times have changed in the last few years. War's had an effect on social conventions and I, for one, am glad it's appropriate for us to be strolling without a chaperone."

Rose smiled.

"Even you have a sparkle in your eyes," Delphi continued. "It's the expectation of a pleasant time in the park with two good-looking men in uniform. We shall be restrained and ladylike when we greet them," Delphi said.

"Indeed, we shall," agreed Rose with a straight expression and then tucked her arm through her sister's. They grinned at each other in unrestrained girlish glee and laughed.

George nudged Michael and nodded in their direction.

Delphi spoke into Rose's ear. "I liked George's accent. He has many interesting experiences to share. He has been to places far flung from this small conventional place."

Rose glanced across at her sister, but there was no time for further thought or conversation as they'd reached the men.

"Ladies, how fine you both look. You have roses in your cheeks. You are well named," Michael said, turning to Rose. She flushed prettily. "Delphi, you are lovely," he added, stating the obvious.

Delphi tossed her head at this but smiled up at him beguilingly before focusing her attention on George.

Rose fully expected some flirtatious crack from her sister, perhaps referring to the fine figure each man cut in their uniforms or how impressed she was with their gallantry or bravery. She was surprised when Delphi demurely asked, "Which way do you think we should go?" She addressed George.

"I don't know the way well enough. Michael, what do you suggest?"

"Beside the river might be muddy still. I propose this way through the flower garden. We could take coffee in the conservatory."

"We shall be ready for that by the time we arrive. It's a chilly wind today," Delphi said. She tucked a stray hair back under her hat with her long, delicate fingers.

Rose's thoughts turned briefly to the same scenario she had shared recently with Thom. He had now returned to Manchester and his secret work in the offices of the military there. She was aware her feelings held an extra exultation this time, though. She felt guilty in her pleasure, but only for a short time. After all, this was only a friendly meeting before the two men went back to their own hell on a grand scale. They deserved some diversion and Rose was determined to be merry, just as Delphi was resolute in her flamboyance and vivacity.

Michael led the way and although Rose hung back for Delphi to walk beside him, she made it clear she would accompany George, the path being too narrow for all four together.

There was silence for a moment until Michael filled the awkwardness with some idle enquiry.

"Is Mr Strong still thinking of buying a motor car? I'd be very interested to see it if he is. The army are using some motor vehicles now."

"I know he would still like to, but it's very expensive to buy and run one. He has had a lot of expense recently with Mama's medical bills."

"There was bit of a quip along those lines in the *Wipers Times*," George said. "Yes, when a man went to the surgery, the doctor said, 'I'll soon have you on your feet.' The patient's friend asked if the doctor had managed it. The patient recounted to his friend, 'He certainly did. I had to sell my car to pay his bill.' I'm not making light of your parents' predicament," George said in a hurry. "It's a comment on the price of things these days, including motor transport, which shouldn't be an indulgence but something for everyone soon."

"I think it will be a luxury for the foreseeable future," Rose said. "Maybe when the situation settles down again, he will be able to pursue his dream."

"Many dreams are on hold currently." Michael looked down at Rose and she nodded her understanding.

"What is the *Wipers Times*?" Delphi glanced up at George.

"It's a brand new paper printed and distributed for the troops in the trenches. A sergeant who had been a printer in peacetime mended a printing press some others salvaged and they made a sample page. The paper itself was named after Tommy slang for Ypres in Belgium. They call the town 'Wipers'. I was lucky to get a copy. A bloke I met had been with someone who was there, and he passed it around. It's full of jokes and comments about the officers."

"You do use some funny words," Delphi said. "I've never heard the word 'bloke' before."

After that the conversation was light and cheerful. By unspoken agreement, no mention at all was made of international affairs. They talked of painting and music, of plays and the latest entertainment at the hall in the town.

They stood and looked at the hellebores growing beside the path, not bright or showy but still flowering in profusion and full of delicate colours. For several moments Michael seemed lost in his own thoughts while Delphi and George moved off along the path. Rose stood silently and waited. He suddenly seemed to come back from some dark place and smiled sheepishly at her.

"I shall paint some of these flowers and send them to you," Rose said.

"They will remind me of this day," Michael responded.

He was back with her and they commented on the birdsong that filled the air as they caught up with the other two.

"They are responding to this sparkling day," Delphi remarked. "They are enjoying it too."

"I will remember and treasure today," George said, looking at Delphi. She refrained from her usual seductive remarks and simply smiled gently. Rose was surprised but made no comment. Michael looked back at her and … was that a wink he passed to Delphi? Seeing the familiarity of it between them, Rose shrivelled inside a little and was quiet. She could see how Michael felt about her lovely, vibrant sister.

I know I am a pale comparison, but I'm a Strong. I shall be strong. I know Thom loves me. Rose raised her chin at the thought.

Michael and George entered the station the next day. It was sunless and sombre. All the colours seemed to merge into the khaki of the crowded concourse. Even the few civilians were in sad hues. The heavy atmosphere hung about most of the people there. The two men were silent, each lost in their own brooding. The long black sleeping snakes beyond the barrier hissed occasionally.

A young wife walked beside her husband, not touching as etiquette demanded and appearing nonchalant.

I know how he feels, and I imagine she is desperate in her suppressed emotion, Michael thought as he watched her face.

Eventually, he said, "I feel like a heavy cloud has enveloped my whole being."

"Me too," George said. "Look at that young buck, though." He nodded at a soldier in tunic, belt, and puttees with a revolver at his side. "Just like we were a few months ago. Oh well, let's get this over with." They hefted their bags and headed for the barrier.

Sitting in a carriage, they spoke in whispers. There was a jolt as the engine took up its load. A young, slim, girlish figure ran parallel to them, waving frantically at someone in the next carriage now that all pretence of self-control was no longer needed. Tears started down her cheeks as she held onto her hat with one hand.

Honour, wounds, hospital, more leave. If we are lucky, peace. What might the future hold? Michael's thoughts ran on.

Much later in the long journey and having changed trains in London, Michael pointed out the window. "This is Kent," he said to George. "See the fruit trees. They look like they are dancing."

"What are those poles for?" As the train rattled along, George nodded at the tall sloping rows joined with strong wires.

"They're for hops. They'll be bobbing with the seed pods after the flowers have been and gone. They're used for beer. Real English bitter, that is. Not that slop you refer to as beer." Michael lightened the mood.

"We're going over there to make sure you can still have your beer, mate. We'll not let the Hun deprive you of that. It's a relief that God will not let Nature lose her loveliness here and that beauty and grace persist somewhere," George said.

"You clearly think it persists where we have just come from too." Michael smiled and winked.

"Delphi, you mean?"

"Did you feel you made some headway there?"

"Do you know, I think I did. I asked her to write and she said she would. She shed a pretty tear as we left yesterday. She tried to hide it, but I saw."

"That was uncharacteristic as far as I know," Michael informed his friend. "She's not a very consistent letter writer I'm afraid, old chum."

"We'll see," said George and he smiled.

The train rumbled rhythmically, lulling the two men until a loud whistle made them jump. The train entered a dark tunnel and they were both back in the hell of No Man's Land in an instant.

CHAPTER 17

A month had passed and, knowing something big was coming, the men said anything to lighten their load. For months now there had been rumours of the 'Big Push'. News from the French was dire and action to relieve the pounding they continued to receive at Verdun was necessary.

Passing by the town of Albert, one of the company said, "There's old Fanny Durack. Some things never change."

"Who?" Michael asked of the young private.

"Fanny," the man repeated. "Sorry, sir. It's only a joke, a cynical witticism, if you will, about the fallen Virgin and Child from the top of the church tower over there. Since 1915 she's been leaning below the horizon and we've renamed her after that champion diver from Australia."

"Here, watch what you say," George reprimanded. "Some people might be offended. That's a sacred image over there and a sordid casualty of this flaming war."

"Sorry, sir," the soldier said and looked sideways at his companion.

"We were away such a short while back last month and we had that training session in Manchester with the maps. It's been so intensive, time's flown by. It feels like we've never been away," Michael said. "Yet it's June already. This push is going to be soon, isn't it?"

"The question is, will it be Flanders or closer to here?" George said.

"I imagine it'll be here. After all, we've been told to go east to this Maricourt place. In the meantime, it'll be the usual round of shelling and raids, I suppose."

"Sounds like we'll not be in the front line yet, though, so it's all good really." George laughed cynically.

As the sun set over the ruins of the town, they moved out. From the top of the hill looking over the terrain ahead, they could see the whole area had been taken over by the army.

"The place is littered with camps and dumps," George said. "Hey, look at that." He pointed.

A huge pillar of smoke and fire rose as if the earth had been split and the centre spewed up in flashes of vermilion, orange and saffron. Even from a distance they saw muck and rocks were flung up high. Gun flashes quivered along the horizon, lasting several minutes.

By mid-June 1916, they were crawling through the mud of No Man's Land yet again and reporting back on the complexity and strength of the German defences.

"The depth of barbed wire around those villages is a real problem," Michael reported to his commanding officer. "It's not a line they have there, it's a fortress. Our information and that of the aerial chaps is that it's twenty or even thirty yards deep."

"We'll need a massive bombardment to deal with that. Those villages are significant and that whole ridge is key to the plan in this sector. The strategy is to break through so that the cavalry can follow."

Michael continued, "About two thousand five hundred yards behind that there is a further line of defences. Here." He indicated on the map between them. "I met with airborne reconnaissance yesterday."

"Good work, Lieutenant."

"Sir."

"Between us, I understand General Rawlinson is using the information from your scouts as we speak. We don't need a repetition of Loos here. There will be an almighty barrage before we go over the top. That should sort the buggers out before we arrive and break the wire sufficiently. Mash their trenches up too, hopefully."

Michael shared some of this conversation with George when he returned to his quarters.

"Let's hope he's correct, then. Trouble is, all this information has been bandied about for months. If I was Jerry, I'd be digging in and be well prepared for a bombardment if I thought one was coming."

"If we deployed gas that would deal with them, even if they are dug in," Michael argued.

"Yeah, mate, but there's always the danger that it'll blow back."

The days ticked by. Troops practised in facsimile trenches. Training seemed all too brief. Michael's troop made forays out to listen at night and sometimes had to stay well into the following morning. By then they were tired, hungry, cold and cramped from hours of non-movement. Men dug new fire trenches in front of existing ones and to form assembly positions and yet more trenches to connect all together. Dozens of deep emplacements were dug for the two-inch and Stokes trench mortars which would then be available during the battle. Then the munitions had to be manhandled through this network and placed ready. There were areas prepared for rations. Prisoner cages were erected. The area was proliferated with men digging and constructing like feverish ants.

Preparation of advanced dressing stations and clearing posts reminded everyone what all this was about. Underneath all the activity was a mix of buzzing excitement and fear. The difference between the two was sometimes paper-thin. Each tried to prepare with resolve and courage, but it didn't always work.

Among all this there was occasional sniper fire.

"It's ironic that today has been a quiet day. June 15th, nothing special, and poor old Pricey was still only nineteen. Just his bad luck. God rest his soul," George said with a sigh.

As the days wore on, men became increasingly optimistic. They had not been involved in the likes of this before.

"We've had skirmishes aplenty and some blokes have copped it, but we were still in training in '15 when Loos was going on. This is the real thing for us now."

"You're right there, Georgie boy," Michael responded. "We'll be in it together too. I'll be watching your back and I know you'll be looking out for me." He slapped his friend across the shoulders. "I couldn't wish for a better companion to be sharing this with. When we get home to Blighty, they'll never believe what we achieved."

The bombardment lasted for six days and nights.

Fountains of grey clay shot up all along the German front lines. Billows of yellow and black smoke could be smelled all night and fire flashed across the sky. The men watched and felt it with a cruel glee. George, in particular, was aware of this and it troubled his soul to see men so far from their normal feelings and thoughts. He understood their savagery, but Michael knew it disturbed his friend deeply. George did what he could to keep them all sane with words of reason, balance and comfort.

Michael imagined the balls of hot iron, the steel rods, and showers of molten earth descending on those young men who happened to be on the enemy's side. The redoubt, at the top of a slight incline, was the first objective. The village of Montauban lay beyond. Further back, larger shells were landing on the *Bricketerie* with its tall chimney situated on the edge of the community. The Hun would be using it for reconnaissance.

"We lay in that scrubland listening to the buggers up there while they watched and picked off young Price and the others."

"Well, it's their turn to be on the receiving end now," George answered. "Oh God, help us all."

The village and the many small woods around it were also getting a pounding.

"Watch over there." George nudged his companion and nodded in the direction of the village. "Look, look!"

A great pink dust cloud erupted, and the ground shook all the way back to where they stood.

"Someone's house has gone up," a young man said.

Heavy shells threw clouds of black smoke three hundred feet into the air. In the middle, red flames shot up relentlessly.

Michael grabbed a moment and continued his diary, which he hoped to send to Rose when all was finished. He could not articulate to himself why it was important that she knew these things.

His memory turned to the day when they had walked in the park. *I imagined I was as free as the dawn*, he thought with some surprise. *But Rose, when I turned and saw you standing there silently while I fought my demons, I think that's when I was captured. Later you smiled with laughter in your eyes. Rose, I was such a fool not to see before and now it's probably too late. You have Thom. Before all this I ran at the thought of settling down, but now...* He put his head in his hands.

June 26th

The nights are the worst because the vibration and noise is relentless. I am optimistic among all this destruction, though. It seems like the end of half the world but it's not my half. Should I feel guilty? I cannot, not when I have seen people I know badly wounded and killed. Surely, we shall prevail. Is our cause not just?

The 27th June 1916 saw Michael and his platoon heading up the lines. The rain trickled down his collar and soaked his clothing. It turned the soil into slippery mud. It was a miserable night and still the cacophony of the bombardment continued.

Is this an indulgence of chaos now? No, I cannot believe that. It is planned with meticulous care. Someone somewhere has the master blueprint. It's not for me to question but to do. I must busy my brain with practicalities not imagined possibilities. Michael was lonely and his thoughts ran unheeded.

After spending a soggy night with little sleep, the next morning the order came through.

"Stand down. Stand down and return to quarters."

"What?"

"Ours is not to question why, ours is but to do…" grumbled someone.

"It's too wet," Michael said. "We would all be slipping about in this mud and orders would be too hard to follow. The aircraft spotters can't go up in this weather, either. We're heading home, boys. Bed and breakfast await us. Be grateful. You get to see another sunset, my friend."

Having built themselves up for it, the compulsory delay leant heavily upon the men.

Michael wrote in a letter to his mother: *I feel tormented and apprehensive. This enforced languor is mean to the spirit.*

Two days later, the soldiers awoke to bright sunshine. Spirits lifted. Michael tore up the letter. The blue sky elevated his motivation. He decided the tone of his previous missive was inappropriate. He would pen another right now and show his mother how positive he felt.

30th June 1916
Dearest Mother,

I feel most optimistic about this next adventure. Everything has been planned meticulously, and I'm sure by the time we reach the German lines there will be no opposition. That has all been taken care of during the previous six days and nights.

The weather here is gloriously warm and sunny. The skylarks are soaring already from the fields and it promises to be a good day.

I need to thank you, Mother, for all you have given me which prepares me to lead my men into the field for this glorious moment.

Please give my very best wishes to Father.

I shall see you again soon, I have no doubt.

Your loving and respectful son,

Michael

That evening they were back in the fire trench. They were set for the 'Big Push': the Battle of the Somme.

CHAPTER 18

July 1916

Dear George,

Thank you for your letter. I hope you are still safe and that when you receive this you will know that I think of you often. It seems such a long time since we last met. I have kept all your letters safely together and they travel with me. Even though we only really know each other through letters (yes, we know each other quite well now) you are close to my heart since you ask.

I have practically finished my initial training already with the Women's Legion. You should see me in my uniform. I look a real sketch in my dress, but the hat is smart. The colour is not so flattering, but I feel quite the ticket even though the greatcoat just about drowns me.

This is your fault, you know. It was you who threw down the proverbial gauntlet when you said I could do something for the dear old country as you are doing. I know you remember that glorious day when we met as I do. I think of it often.

The first group of women are due to go to France at the end of this month. There will only be fourteen of them, but I have high hopes of following in their footsteps shortly after that.

You never know, we may meet up at some point. Wouldn't that be tickety-boo? That's a new word I've discovered. Isn't it lovely?

Our seniors are not called officers but are Officials or Controllers. We have Administrators and their Assistants. I shall be a Controller one day, you wait and see. The different ranks are the same as in the proper army, but they won't have women with the same titles as you lot!

Napoleon said, I think it was in 1915, 'An army marches on its stomach', so I am to be posted and will probably be peeling onions and mashing potatoes, but at least our kitchen will feed the men better than the old military cooks did, you can be sure of that.

This is certainly a step on from baking cakes in the local hall for soldiers at the front. Do you remember that recipe for Trench Cake? No eggs and vinegar with baking soda to make it rise. You never did tell me if it was edible, which probably means it wasn't.

We are going to Dartford for the final part of our training before hopefully coming to France. Papa is most unhappy about all this. He has written to me about it endlessly. I think he even wrote to my Controller, although nothing must have come of that. I shall not be deterred.

In the meantime, George dear, keep safe PLEASE. I send you my tender love and keep yours locked in my heart.

From your (good, hardworking) Delphi

Rose now worked in Manchester. She could not stay at home knitting and baking any longer. The war effort needed her, and her keen brain seemed the best thing to use. She knew she was not physically suited to a factory job. Her eyesight let her down, for a start. Truthfully and somewhat guiltily, she could not bear to work with munitions and develop the yellow tinge to her skin that the 'canary girls' had from the prolonged exposure to sulphuric acid.

She worked in an office and dealt with the forms and papers which resulted from all the soldiers killed or seriously wounded. She often had to meet next of kin and help them through the bureaucracy of finding their loved one's personal possessions and sort out any pay that was owed.

Right now, it was her lunchbreak. She swung along the street, managing to take pleasure in the world outside the building in which she laboured. Her face was lit with inner happiness. She had received another letter from Michael, as had Delphi. At least she knew he was still safe. She was certain that Delphi only wrote to him because she wanted news of George. Michael only mentioned her sister quite incidentally to Rose in the letters she got. He must be hurting badly at Delphi's shallow callousness towards him. Rose understood but was still sure he needed news of her sister. It must be like a wound that wouldn't heal.

"My dear, you look lovely," Thom said.

He shook her hand in a way that would not compromise her in public. Ensuring she was placed on the inside of the pavement and with his walking stick in his other hand, Thom strolled along the street with her towards their lunch destination. Rose matched her step to his uneven gait as best she could.

"How is your work going? I know you can give me no details, of course," she said.

"Well enough, and I suspect there will be some very long sessions coming imminently. We are very close to making a breakthrough with the project. I may have to go down to Dorset soon. We are designing a modification that we shall need to put to the test."

Dorset! That seemed to confirm her guess that he was working on the new tanks that Rose had heard rumours about while at work. They were expected to secure an edge in defeating the enemy. They never spoke of it. Rose was trusted to be very circumspect about the things she heard. Thom had signed papers to ensure utmost secrecy.

"This confounded war!" Rose spoke with feeling. "Anything you can do to give us some dominance is invaluable."

"Oh, Rose, you are so good for me and my confidence. I promise to do my bit and work hard for this country. Dear Rose, I think so highly of you."

"I know, but Thom, please say no more. I can give you nothing further, at least until we see the end of all this conflict. Things are too complicated and uncertain."

"I know, my dear." He sighed. "I live in hope that you might come to love me as I do you."

Rose stopped walking and turned to face him. "I have a great respect for you."

"We will speak intimately no more." He smiled kindly down at her and she wished she could feel more than she did. Perhaps if or even when the war was finally over, she would make a decision. Things were so puzzling. She loved Michael. He adored her beautiful sister, she was sure. Delphi clearly had fallen head over heels in love with George. His maturity seemed to complement her vivacity and mercurial nature. Here was Thom offering her so much. If only she could get this silly infatuation out of her heart. Perhaps she should settle for security over profound love. Maybe that intensity was not for her.

"What of your work? Is the travelling still working out well?"

"It makes a much longer day, but I'd rather travel here and back each day than stay in a greasy flat somewhere. The work is not difficult. It fluctuates between being somewhat dull with the filling in of endless forms and being extremely upsetting when I have to speak with relatives of the fallen."

"I know you do it with compassion, Rose," Thom said and gave her arm a little pat.

"I had to talk with the parents of a young private the other day. They came to collect the rest of his pay and his effects. He was underage, as many are. It reminded me of Hector. I do hope he is safe."

"Have you heard from him again?"

"No, but Michael said he had seen him last month. He's still a runner and it is beyond good fortune that he has made it this far. It is such a dangerous job."

"You still write to Michael, then?" Thom asked the question with tentative concentration.

"Yes, just as a friend, as you know. It is Delphi that he would have, but as I said before, she has developed real feelings for George Dight."

July 1916
Dear Rose,

How are you, my dear sister? I am having such a zippy time here in Dartford. The dormitory in which we sleep is very basic and not very warm, but the girls are generally good company. There is just one who thinks she is better than the rest of us, but she is struggling with some aspects of the work. Ha ha! I can hardly believe I am putting up with these conditions and actually enjoying it. Me, of all people!

I feel sure I shall be going to France soon. Rumours are rife that we shall be quite close to the front, and I am excited at the prospect. Wouldn't it be fun if I bumped into you know who? He writes to me often, and I would really like to see him again to verify what we write to each other. What if he doesn't really love me? What if I don't really love him? That's more the point. His letters reveal much about him and I certainly was attracted to him when we met, but it's not the same, is it?

I am learning a lot about quantities and costs when feeding groups from a patrol to a battalion. It muddles the mind unless I concentrate, but I got a 'well done' from our Controller so that was good and one in the eye for Miss Know Nothing. I felt sorry for her, though, and offered to help her out which she accepted grudgingly. She owes me something now.

How are you and the work you are doing? Have you seen Thom recently? You should take pity upon him.

I miss you all. Give my love to Mama and everyone there. Tell Izzy I love her too. I'm not sure she always knew that. I have been mean sometimes, I know.

Your loving sister,
Delphi

Rose considered all that her sister had said. It was a genuine surprise to hear Delphi speak so of Izzy. Perhaps the knowledge of her departing soon for France had given her cause for sober thought. It might be dangerous, and Delphi wrote as if she appreciated that. To consider one's own mortality at such a tender age was a huge thing. Most of the young men of her generation wondered about their own demise too, she was sure. Michael must have these thoughts and self-doubts.

Oh, I hope he is safe. Rose's head sunk into her hands as she sat. *I'll go mad.*

She had a sinking feeling. In the depths of her soul, Rose knew something was very wrong but not what it could be.

CHAPTER 19

The Somme, 1916

The night had been interminable. The noise of the artillery was deafening. Everyone had to shout directly into their neighbour's ear to be heard. The trench was so crowded there was only room to stand and lean against the side, and the rumbling explosions shook the ground upon which they stood. Each man was weighed down with his rifle and bayonet, wire cutters, a shovel, two days' rations, an oil sheet, Mills bombs, 150 rounds of ammunition, two extra bandoliers containing 60 rounds each and a bag of ten bombs. Time seemed to stand still.

"I want a raiding party to go out to capture a German prisoner as soon as there is a break in the barrage," the Major said. "Any information in advance of the attack will be invaluable."

After a short while, thirty-nine men crawled across the mud towards the enemy trenches. There was a spit of fire but that was all those behind heard, and no one wanted to put their head above the parapet to see. The men awaited the return of the party.

After listening, on their return the patrol reported the absence of all Germans.

"The trenches over there were deserted and the wire cut," a corporal recounted with awe in his tone. "Where are they all?"

Just one lad was killed on the way back by a sniper's lucky bullet.

"'Ere, that's good, innit?" A young private's face was expectant in his optimism as he stood next to Michael. "Only one copped it. That's good odds."

"Yeah, it's good, lad," Michael answered.

There were some moments of silence straight after daybreak that morning. A skylark rose from somewhere nearby. Unseen, the men were aware of its flight by the shrill sound of its calling as it flew higher and higher, oblivious to the forthcoming pandemonium.

Men scribbled their final notes with pencils that were wearing low and dropped them into the sandbag that a Private struggled to carry through the morass of men.

Beyond the trench, the silence continued.

An hour to go.

The rum was issued at 6.45 a.m., just as the mist lifted. Michael knew the Liverpool lads were on one flank and the French on the other. He imagined the same scenario continuing for miles on either side.

Half an hour to go. Men stamped and shifted.

Quarter of an hour to go. Someone cleared their throat and another coughed.

Ten minutes to go.

Two minutes to go.

At 7.29 a.m. precisely, a flare went up and whistles blew. In the distance, a Scots piper could be heard. The sound meant to be stirring but it was mournful.

Suddenly shouts and growls arose from the men as they urged themselves into a frenzy. Michael and his patrol were among the first up the ladders and over the top. Two hundred and fifty men formed a wave, each about a yard apart. A vast number awaited their turn to climb the steps, to form subsequent waves. Many had a 'woody' hanging from their lips in an attempt to calm their nerves as they inhaled the smoke.

This is such a beautiful sunny morning, Michael thought. *It's surreal.*

The initial shouts soon disappeared as men began to concentrate. Their objective was the north face of the Glatz Redoubt.

"It's hard going, isn't it, sir? All the shell holes and loose soil make it tough," a young lad panted.

"Keep low, lad," Michael encouraged him.

He heard dull thuds as bullets started to hit the soil around him.

"Aargh!"

Michael turned to see the boy had fallen and red oozed into the soil at his side.

After two hundred yards of toiling uphill and ducking, the second wave caught up with them. Men fell around him and Michael dived into a shell hole. He landed next to the body of a soldier who looked as if he was asleep. There was no sign of any damage. He felt the boy's neck for a pulse and as he withdrew his fingers, he realised the back of his head was missing and blood had flowed into the soil. It covered Michael's hands and he shuddered as he tried to wipe them on the ground and down his trousers. He rolled away and screwed his eyes tight shut. He felt sick.

He turned over again and looked up at the sky. It was wide and so blue it took his breath away. For a moment all the noise, all the horror, disappeared. He gazed up until his eyes were dry and sore. Then he looked again at his hands and was brought back to reality.

He scrambled to the edge and poked his head up to see. So many men had fallen. Explosions and belches of soil ahead showed him where the enemy trenches were.

I'm no hero, he realised and lowering his head, he closed his eyes. *I'm between hell and more hell here. I want to stay hidden.* He felt tears prick his eyes and dashed his sleeve over his face, spreading muck and sweat.

His thoughts turned to his recent leave. *I need to see Rose again.* He pictured her calming grey eyes. He thought of the flash of fire in Delphi's, but then his mind returned to the peace of Rose's demeanour.

He took a deep breath. *No! I need to go forwards. I can't let the others do this without me, and I couldn't return home and face them there either if I stay here.*

He scrambled up and over. His weariness and the weight of his equipment slowed his progress before he stood again and lumbered across the ground.

"Move up on the left," an officer yelled before pitching forwards. He never gave another order.

"Hey, are you okay mate?" Michael recognised George's voice, although his features were obscured by mud.

"Never better, pal. Nearly there," Michael answered with grim determination.

"Watch out, here they come!" George yelled.

Michael pointed his rifle in front of him. Its bayonet, still clean, glinted in the sun and then he realised that dozens of German soldiers were running through his lines with their hands up. A shot rang out to Michael's left, making him duck, and one of the Germans fell.

"That's for my brother at Loos," someone shouted. There were more shots and screams. Michael and those close to him didn't look back.

"We were told to take no prisoners," a gruff voice roared, and a coarse laugh disappeared into the mêlée.

They all charged on and, upon reaching the German trench, flung themselves in.

"Not much of this left," George said, looking at the shattered walls and wreckage.

Bodies littered the way and papers floated around in the smoke-filled air. The stench was terrific, but Michael stepped over the debris of war and focused upon what lay ahead.

They proceeded along the trench.

"God, this is nerve-racking," Michael whispered as he crept forward, ducking low and peering around a corner where the trench doglegged. "Their construction is the same as ours."

"Yes, well, these doglegs would stop a blast travelling along a great length."

Finding empty silence greeting them, they continued to the next corner with stealth. Behind they heard their comrades entering the system. Ahead they could see the black entrance of a dugout. There was a scrap of hessian hanging by a crooked edge. As they arrived, they saw steps descended.

"What do we do? They could be waiting for us," George said. "Have you got any number 5s left? We could lob one in and that would finish them off." There was urgency in his whispered enquiry.

"That would bring the whole lot crashing in, and if there's any intelligence in there it'd be lost," Michael reasoned.

George swore.

"We might as well rush them. They must know we're here. Perhaps surprise will confound them just long enough. I'll go first, you follow, and we'll hope to get one on them," Michael said optimistically.

"Okay, if this is it, it's a lovely day for it and God bless you for your friendship, cobber."

"You and your words. What's wrong with good old English?" Michael smiled. "It's been good, my friend," he added before turning back to face the dark hole and the steps down which seemed to go on forever.

He advanced. One, two, three, four steps made of wood. He paused and, realising how tense he was, he took a deep breath. Five, six, seven steps. Pause. Eight, nine steps. A quick glance down and he realised there were four more.

"It's so deep. No wonder they survived the bombardment. These walls are solid concrete," George whispered behind him.

Clinging to the wall, Michael counted in his head. *One, two, three…*

Yelling at the top of his voice, he leaped down the last few steps and crouched to the side of the doorway. George shouted too and flung himself to the other side.

"*Nicht schießen, nicht schießen.*" A stocky boy hid behind a chair and his pudgy face peeped out. Putting his hands up, he shouted in panic and stood. "*Ich bin allein. Sie alle gingen.*" He indicated he was alone. He pointed up the steps.

Michael shoved his bayonet at the boy's chest and gave it a push. His finger quivered on the trigger of the rifle. The boy was trembling. He backed up.

"*Nicht, bitte nicht.*" He flinched and shook his head. His eyes shone with moisture.

Not fully understanding but getting the gist of the boy's meaning, Michael nodded at the doorway. The boy shot up the steps and clambered over the remains of the parapet. They watched his retreating figure as he stumbled towards the Allied line with hands held high, crying as he went.

"You might regret that," George said.

"He was just a spotty youth," Michael said. "He could probably have killed me as we entered, but he was too scared to even shit himself. Have a look around. Are there any papers, anything of interest?"

"I dunno, mate, but there are some good souvenirs, though," George said. "Look, they didn't take their coats. They left in a right rush. Those buttons will fetch a pretty penny back near the coast. Those guys are missing all this fun. They'll be only too keen to buy a few choice pieces."

"That's certainly true, but let's get the info first. Have a scout around, Georgie boy, and then we'll hack a few buttons off for you."

CHAPTER 20

July 1916
My dearest Rose,

Rose gasped in the silence of her room. She became breathless and her heart trembled. Never before had Michael addressed her so. Then her blood, in that moment so warm, froze and her legs gave way. She sank down onto her bed. His information was devastating.

Of course, I cannot say where we are, but I have some terrible news for you. I am so sorry. I saw Hector last month as I told you. He was exhilarated and full of his army life then, but I must sadly tell you now that he has died. I cannot break it to you more gently. I know he had a false name here and it is unlikely that your family will hear through conventional means. I do not want to add to your distress by giving you the details of his passing, but I can say that he died in action and was not in any way a disgrace to your family's name.

My dear Rose, it will be left to you to share this information with your parents. I was unsure whether to write directly to them and instead I have left you with this burden, for which I am sorry too. It will not be an easy task. He was calling himself Harry Stone. Your parents will need this information if they are to trace him and claim their relationship.

My sincere thoughts and prayers are with you. Again, I am so sorry to impart this terribly sad news and not be there to support you in any way.

Yours in sorrow,
Michael

Rose sat for several moments, her mind numb. How on earth was she to share this with her parents? Then, in a frenzy, she scribbled a note back. All thoughts of Michael's intimacy were gone.

Dear Michael,

Thank you for letting me know first of Hector's passing. Please do not spare my sensibilities. I need to have the details of it. I must understand and this I can do only by knowing every fact. I shall say nothing to Mama and Papa until I have heard from you with more information. Perhaps that will help me to tell them.

Yours in sincerity,

Rose

Putting on her coat and hat, Rose hurried down the stairs and out to the post office. The note would reach Michael in two or three days. The postal service to the forces overseas was remarkably efficient.

As she hurried down the lane, she noticed none of the blossoms or the burgeoning leaves. She didn't take heed of any birdsong. Her artist's eyes did not observe the rippling, sea-green barley this time. She thought solely of how she might inform her parents. She decided to wait until she had all the facts. It would be hard to keep this awful news to herself and remain outwardly calm, but she was strong.

"Rose, I hope you are not sickening for something," Mrs Strong said later that day.

"No, Mama. I'm just very tired. It must be all the travelling."

"Are you quite well, Rose?" This time it was Izzy asking, the next morning.

"I shall be fine," Rose replied. "I've had a difficult time at work. I had to speak to the parents of a very young lad who died when they came for his effects." This was so close to the truth that she turned away to hide the glisten in her eyes.

She remained in her room as much as possible when not at work and it wasn't long until the response came from Michael, for which she had been waiting with morbid anticipation.

My very dear Rose,

I have been thinking of your inner calm and it grieves me to impart this information that you have demanded of me. I fear it will destroy your peace for some time, and I would have liked so much to be there to help you through this.

Hector was asked to take a message to the HQ. It is not unusual for runners to leave the safety of trenches in favour of speed. He must have done this, and a sniper got him.

I went to see him in the stationary hospital. He received basic first aid in the dressing station, but due to the nature of the battle it was a while before he obtained the full attention of a surgeon.

Rose winced. She had the image of her brother lying wounded, hot, thirsty and alone. Images of his young face as she had last seen him popped into her mind. No doubt he was changed. A young man, now with a wealth of experience about which she could only guess.

Oh Rose, he was delirious with a high temperature and very poorly. He received devastating injuries to his left side. He did not know me but was raving and sweating profusely. I sat with him for a while and wiped his face until my duty called for my return.

Rose took a deep breath and closed her eyes. *I hope someone was there to take tender care of him.* She pictured the nurses being so busy and tired that visits to Hector's bedside would be limited. Thank goodness Michael had become such a good friend to her family.

I returned the following day and was there when he passed. He slept deeply by then. I don't know if they gave him something to make him calm. Maybe not, because just before he died, he opened his eyes and pulled the biggest, shiniest smile you could imagine.

Again, Rose closed her eyes. Tears escaped from the corners. The letter dropped to her lap, but only for a moment.

Dearest Rose, take comfort that he was peaceful at the end. I cannot imagine how you will break this news to your parents. Take comfort, too, in the knowledge that he was doing what he wanted. The last time we met he was radiant and enjoying his role in this conflict. Some chaps do love it here, believe it or not. They take glee in the camaraderie and excitement and seem not to mind the discomfort and mud. I cannot understand that, but it is true.

Please write soon and let me know how you fare. My thoughts are with you all.

Michael

X

A kiss at the end! Rose was in turmoil and the tears fell unchecked at last. She sobbed and heaved at the waste of it all. She cried at the loneliness and futility. The world would never be as it had been and she mourned that too, even though when rational thought returned, she would be vaguely aware that some elements of that were good.

Eventually the waterfall subsided. She splashed her face to calm her tired eyes and gathering up the pages of Michael's letter, she went in search of her parents.

Thankfully, her father was in his study when she knocked. He spent a lot of time there these days. He was reading a newspaper. He smiled at her when she responded to his call to enter, but she could not reciprocate, and his smile faded away. A frown replaced it as he saw her tired, red-rimmed eyes.

"Papa, I need to speak with you. I have news."

One look at her face and he knew she had something terrible to impart.

"I have a letter from Michael Redfern. He has information about Hector." She gulped in some air. "Papa, it is not good."

He took the letter and read. Rose's tears returned and she wiped her eyes in the silence.

"Thank you for your calm courage, Rose. It supports us all well. Come here, child."

As he stood, she sank into his embrace with relief. She felt the rough fabric of his jacket and smelled the pipe smoke that clung to his person. Seldom did any of them receive this level of intimacy from a parent.

"I shall remain here for a moment and then go in search of Mama. We shall endure together somehow. We owe him that much, and this I shall impress upon her. Leave now, Rose, my dearest."

"Yes, Papa."

Rose stood quietly in the hall looking out of the window when her papa passed. He placed his hand on her shoulder, just briefly. She did not turn. The door to the sitting room was open. Her mother was seated. Sewing was in her lap, but Rose saw that she was staring at nothing.

As Rose left to remount the stairs, she heard a soul-wrenching howl from the room below.

CHAPTER 21

Rose wrote to Delphi with the news of their brother. In Delphi's reply, she told her she was returning for a short break before leaving for France.

My feelings are so mixed. I am loath to leave you all, especially now, but at the same time I am full of anticipation. I am sure Mama and Papa will not be happy with it.

I am very much looking forward to seeing you all again, even if only for a short time.

Rose finished work early the afternoon that Delphi returned so that she could meet the train and welcome her sister.

"It seems an age since I was here," Delphi said after they had hugged. "I remember all that fear and nausea as I waited in the station when I left. Did you feel like that, Rose, before you went to Oxford?"

"I do remember being very excited, but nervous too," Rose said.

The sisters appraised each other. Rose could see a maturing of Delphi's features, but she was no less stunning. Where had she attained such looks? No wonder Michael as well as George seemed besotted with her. Rose was aware that her own appearance was far more ordinary. There she stood in the unflattering black that mourning dictated. It washed the colour from her face.

"Rose, you look very pretty today, despite the horrid colour of your clothing. Your eyes are shining. Are you happy, dearest?"

"Happy to see you again," Rose replied with a smile. "As for the rest, life continues here much as before, except that Mama hardly ever comes to the drawing room these days."

"How *are* things at home?"

"Mama took to her bed again and seems very frail," Rose said. "She has taken it very hard, and Papa is unable to help her more. He is patient, and I know he is suffering too. He blames himself for not ensuring Hector remained at home."

"Well, it wasn't his fault! Hector was determined. After all, it wasn't the first time he tried to go, and Papa was successful in preventing him then. He became more devious, that's all."

"Yes, you're right," Rose agreed. "Now tell me of you. What have you been doing?"

"Oh, Rose, you should see us when we are in the kitchens practising making pounds and pounds of stuff. It's a hoot sometimes. One girl put a whole packet of salt instead of sugar into the crumble mix. She got a good ticking off from our Controller. She's a real tartar of a woman. I shall have more compassion and understanding when I'm one." Delphi raised her eyebrows and gave Rose a sideways look.

"What of your living conditions?"

"Sometimes it has been *so* cold, but we manage. There is only one bathroom and it's in a shed. Can you imagine? We have to go through the coal cellar to get to it. Getting our hair dry is the main problem, and putting it up under the hats can be tricky. I really think I should cut it all short. It would be so much more practical. What do you think of this uniform, hey?" Delphi twirled with her head on one side and her hand holding her hat. "Don't I look an absolute fright?"

Rose had to admit she looked delectable even in the awful khaki uniform. The dress was shapeless but for the narrow leather belt.

"I shall be a Controller one day, you wait and see. They wear a fitted jacket with epaulettes and badges. The shirt is a paler colour and the tie dark. They had to take up my coat so that it was regulation eight and a half inches from the ground. I think it used to belong to someone in the regular army. It's so vast."

"I cannot believe you've done this," Rose said. "I cannot imagine you without your comforts at all."

"Well, to tell you the truth, Rose, it has been a shock, but I wanted to do my bit, especially after George told me some of what he does. It doesn't seem right to be sitting at home twiddling our thumbs, does it?"

"No, but you didn't have to go and enrol with the Women's Legion."

"I must admit it isn't quite what I expected, as I say." She grimaced. "But now that I'm in I can't really get out of it, and it will be fun to go to France and see a foreign country."

Rose wondered if Delphi had been caught up in a fictitious glamour, as had so many young men. Then her sister confounded her thoughts with her next comment.

"It's not a false allure, Rose. You know me. It's got to be the whole hog or nothing at all and besides, I need to see what our boys are enduring. I need to be part of it. Anyway, tell me of you. What is your work like? More importantly, give me all the gossip about you and Thom, and I do mean *all*."

They had left the station. They headed across the enormous forecourt, watching for traffic, for it was always busy with horses and traps and motor cars and omnibuses turning.

"Mostly my job is dealing with paperwork. Since spring of 1916 it has been non-stop. So many men lost, and so many relatives to see."

"And Thom?" Delphi would not be sidetracked. "Come on, Rose, out with it. Are you going to accept him in the end?"

"Delphi, I can commit to nothing while this war continues. He is moving to Dorset imminently and I have no idea for how long." Rose avoided the penetrating looks from her sister.

"You'll see him before he goes, won't you?"

"I shall meet him at the weekend and after that, who knows."

They boarded the motor omnibus and all intimate talk ceased for a time.

"Delphi, I really do not think you should go to France, my dear child," said Mr Strong.

"Papa, I can hardly not go. All of us are going."

"Not if I say no." Mr Strong was sitting in a leather chair in his study. He spent nearly all his spare time in seclusion there these days. By his side on the small occasional table was his pipe and tobacco tin, forgotten while they spoke.

"You wouldn't, Papa, surely you wouldn't." Delphi was seriously worried for the first time. She had always managed to persuade her father with her pretty smiles and wheedling ways. "What on earth would people say? They would think I was simply taken with an idea and that when it came to it, I funked it."

"Perhaps you were just thinking of idealism, my dear. It will not be thrilling and certainly not elegant. It will be incredibly hard work, squalid and exacting, not to say dangerous."

"I know, Papa. Well, from my training I have a good idea of what to expect. I need to do this, *please*."

"What of your mother? This could be disastrous for her."

"Oh, Papa, that is not fair. This war is so much greater than any one person, no matter how strongly I love her. I have to go, I do!"

"Well, you have certainly grown up, my child. Have you truly thought this through?"

"Papa, I have."

He sighed and put his head in his hands. Delphi knelt at his knee, sensing a capitulation, taking no joy in her victory but being intensely relieved.

"Very well, Delphi, but take no risks and please come back to us."

"Thank you, dearest Papa. Thank you."

He stood and took the unprecedented step of raising her to her feet and giving her a hug. This, more than anything, brought tears to her eyes.

Rose smiled as Thom approached with his familiar irregular gait.

He is uncomplicated and gentle. He is a good man and I could do so much worse, she thought as he arrived. Her mind reverted to the conversation with Delphi. Clearly her sister thought she should stop prevaricating and decide in favour of marriage to Thom.

"My dear, it is always so good to see you," he said as he kissed her hand in a chaste and gentlemanly fashion. They headed for the tearoom, a respectable distance between them. "You look lovely today," he added.

Rose looked up at him appraisingly. He was slim as well as tall, and his civilian clothes were fashionably cut but not dandified.

In the tearoom, he ordered for them both and Rose had further opportunity to study him. His dark eyes sparkled, and his curly hair had grown a little, becoming unruly again. His countenance was open and honest, if not particularly handsome. He was very dear to her. Was that enough?

Rose swallowed and pretended to straighten her skirt as she remembered his last letter.

She had just thought she might be coming to a decision regarding Thom when Michael crept into her mind and destroyed all calm thoughts.

"I don't know how long I shall be gone." Thom was speaking and Rose suddenly realised she had missed the first part of his sentence.

"I'm so sorry, Thom, I didn't catch what you said."

"I was saying I am off to Dorset in the middle of this week coming."

"Of course, I hope all goes well for you and for the project."

"Please write to me and allow me to send you news too." He leaned across the table towards her and spoke quietly. "I was wondering if I might take with me some hope that you have considered your future with me, Rose. I did not mean to propose marriage to you here, in a café of all places." He smiled at her.

Rose looked around her, feeling trapped. She took a gulp of air. This was so unfair of her. She could not string him along. "Thom, I like you immensely, and of course we shall exchange letters." She paused.

Before she could continue, he spoke. "Rose, that word 'like' says it all. I understand, truly I do. I hoped you would grow to love me as I do you, my dear."

"Thom, I cannot. I'm so sorry."

"I recognise that, really." He reached across the table and took her hand. "There is no thunder in your heart and no fire in your eyes. Not for me."

"I wish you well with all my heart. You are a dear man." She hung her head then raised her chin and looked him in the eye. "Thom, it cannot be." There was nothing more to be said.

CHAPTER 22

Delphi landed in France after an interminable journey through a very choppy English Channel. She was exhausted by the time they had crossed the sea and arrived at their temporary billet. She was one among a group of twenty-eight women, and each hut would be shared by seven people. They had been told the toilets were in a block some distance from the huts.

Numerous other wooden buildings with tin roofs and a town of tents of differing sizes formed the camp. Between these was a network of wooden walkways intended to make passage easier through the mud, which still managed to ooze between the boards. Smoke belched from some place off to one side, but Delphi did not recognise the smell and had no wish to explore. Horses stamped in a long low stable. They smelled too and blew little clouds of steam into the cool evening air. Men stomped across patches of ground in all directions. There seemed to be no pattern to any of it, and the camp looked huge to Delphi's inexperienced eyes. They entered their hut.

"I thought the training accommodation was basic, but look at the gaps through there." One girl pointed to where the window frame met the rough wood planking of the walls.

"I'm so weary at the moment I don't care for anything else," Delphi said. "Just let me collapse here and go into a coma."

"Right, ladies." A supervisor had arrived. "Look lively and get this room tidy."

They all groaned but heaved themselves up to stand at the ends of the metal bedsteads.

"No one is to do anything until everything is spotless and things are put away. You have half an hour and I shall return to inspect the place."

Following her diatribe, the Supervisor turned to leave. The girl in the bed opposite Delphi's pulled a face behind the officer's back and several others giggled. Delphi imagined the Supervisor was fully aware of what was thought of her. At any rate, she turned.

"I have been here long enough to know it's my job to maintain good discipline, and you girls are new to France. If you are to survive the rigours ahead, you need to develop a hard shell of protection. Not only will your nerves be tested but your emotions too. As yet you're ignorant of what lies before you, and you'll need to steel yourselves. You may need my help, so have a care."

"Yes, ma'am," the girls chorused, and most had the grace to look shamefaced.

The Supervisor spun round, banging the door behind her. Then it re-opened and her head poked around it. Silence greeted her. "Oh yes, by the way, which one of you is Strong? Controller Swaine wants to see you as soon as you have done as I've asked, so you better look sharp here."

Delphi raised her eyebrows at the girl next to her but shrugged before turning to cover the metal springs of the bedstead with the thin mattress and coarse covers provided.

Delphi knocked on the Controller's office door, having asked directions.

"Come," a voice rang out. Delphi pushed the wooden door, and with her head held high she marched in and stood to attention.

"Ah, Strong." Controller Swaine smiled at her and placed her pencil down beside her papers. "Stand easy. It has been noted that you are a good team player."

"Thank you, ma'am."

"Also, you show a depth of understanding about training so far. It's with the advice of your superiors that I think you will do very well as Unit Administrator. It's a promotion that you have earned."

"Oh, ma'am, thank you."

"You'll be supporting the Quartermaster's area of responsibility. Sourcing supplies will be taxing at times, but I'm confident you are able to engender the support of those under you. You have the brain and good sense to be able to work well at this level."

"I shall endeavour to do an excellent job, ma'am."

"You've earned it, Strong. Here, take these and get them sewn onto your uniform tonight. That will be all."

Delphi took the new badges, stood to attention, saluted and turned. Once outside, she skipped and smiled, and jumping a puddle she hurried along the wooden walkway back to her hut.

Two days later, Delphi paused her work to look through the mud-splattered window. There was a racket going on outside. What she saw made her jaw drop. A man was approaching the camp on a very rickety bicycle. As he came, he waved and shouted to those he passed.

"I know him!" Delphi shouted to the silent walls and she rushed out onto the narrow veranda.

Several of the men pointed towards her and the man on the bike skidded to a halt using his heels.

"Blasted thing has no brakes." He grinned. "Poxy bloke never told me that when I borrowed it."

"George, what are you doing here? I can't believe it. How amazing!"

"I heard the Women's Legion had arrived and when I asked around, I thought there was a good chance you might be here. I've only got an hour or so and then I have to be back." He threw his transport to the ground without ceremony and jumped across to Delphi's area amidst cheers from some of those around. "Can you get away or should I come in?"

"You better come in."

"I'll leave the door open to preserve your reputation," George said as he removed his cap.

"How are you, where are you stationed and what's going on?" Her questions cascaded out. "It's so good to see you after all the letters we've shared."

"Delphi, if only you knew how I have longed for this meeting."

He stepped sideways so the door was sheltering him, and she stepped towards him.

Next she was against his chest and inside the sanctuary of his arms. She turned her head and his lips came down to meet hers in a long and eager kiss. Briefly surfacing for air, they kissed again with tempestuous fervour.

"Oh, my girl, are you sure about this?"

"George, I've never been more certain. Before I wasn't sure. Letters are a poor substitute, but as soon as I saw you on that ridiculous bicycle I knew."

He stayed for an hour, during which time they talked and talked. Finally, the pressures of the situation took hold again.

Behind the door he held her strongly and kissed her forehead, her neck, her lips and finally, moving onto the veranda once more in sight of the company, he raised her hand and kissed that before he left.

She watched him go and before the bend in the track took him from her, he turned, wobbled violently and waved.

Closing the office door behind her and leaning against it, she thanked her lucky stars that he had found her in the hut working on her own this morning.

CHAPTER 23

The 19th Manchesters were still resting when George returned.

More men had now joined Michael and George in the trench system that had belonged to the enemy. Fire steps were reversed from one side of the trench to the other and repairs done to make it ready for the next stage of the battle. The narrow walkway was crowded with movement. Bodies were cleared, the wounded moved and prisoners marched along. Then the order came to take the village ahead to help relieve pressure on the 18th's men. The barrage that had aimed to destroy this side of the small community aimed further north.

"Heads down, men," Michael shouted. He only had three of his own men left. "Wait for this lot first." He referred to the guns doing their best to smash the enemy ahead of their own advance.

"That's forty minutes now," someone shouted. "I 'ate this waiting game. Let's get on and get it over wiv."

"I'm so thirsty," a young lad moaned.

"I can't carry any more," another said and collapsed to the ground.

"Keep your chin up." Michael addressed a passing private who hauled himself along the trench.

It was young Percy Rowbotham. His face was haggard with pain and Michael glanced down and saw the reason. His leg was soaked with blood as he heaved himself along with the help of a stout staff. A cigarette hung from the corner of his mouth, but he was unable to drag on it as he sobbed with tears of suffering and rage.

"You might be out of it, but we'll finish it for you, never fear," Michael added, trying to sound brave for himself as much as for those around him.

A screening barrage was raised as Michael prostrated himself in the dust and watched.

"It's to confuse the German Forward Artillery Observation," he explained to a lad who lay alongside him. "See, it's bringing wasted shellfire down over there instead of here." He took a deep breath. "Here we go. Come on, men!" he shouted and scrambled up and over yet again.

They had to cross another trench which was wide and deep, and their passage was hindered by even more traffic of wounded and prisoners moving through this.

The noise was immense. The smell was intense. The men were exhausted and thirsty already. The land was pitted and gouged, making progress slow. Eventually, men from other brigades joined them. Scots, Liverpool men, and others from Manchester all pushed forwards as one dense mass.

"Nearly there, nearly there!" Michael yelled, but no one could hear him.

"Aargh!" Shouts and moans emanated from some while others silently dropped as indiscriminate shrapnel shells continued to do their deadly work. The men moved steadfastly towards the false security of the village ruins.

Concentrate, don't look at them. You cannot help them. Steady, advance, walk, steady advance, walk, walk, walk. Michael's thoughts ran in a circle. *No end to this grind. Walk, walk, walk. Keep your eyes on that building.*

Finally, he reached the objective. Some Germans, more than a hundred, ran out with their hands in the air and passed the Allies, dazed and dusty.

By the time Michael reached the centre of the village, it was clear that it was now deserted. The plan of streets he had tried so hard to memorise during recent training was unrecognisable. The houses and roads were so damaged. Orange brick dust and choking cordite fumes hung in the air and coated the men.

"I'm parched," said Michael. "In here." He beckoned and a group of men followed him into a ruined building where they collapsed in a corner. It was several moments before they had the energy to delve around and find their water bottles.

Michael closed his eyes. An image of Rose sprang into his mind. Dear, sweet, loyal Rose with her cloud of wayward hair and calm grey eyes.

What wouldn't I give to be at home now? he thought. *I need her quiet strength. She has Thom, though. Probably no room for me when I eventually get away from all this. What a fool I've been.*

He wanted to cry out in anguish for the fallen men; for the muck and stench they were all enduring; for the noise and clamour that never seemed to halt; for the endless horror of it all. Tears squeezed into the corners of his eyes, but he kept them closed and put his head back. He concentrated hard so they didn't flow down his face.

This won't do. Such ignominy to weep. What a feeble chap you're being. I hope beyond all else that George has made it, too. His thoughts tumbled together as he sat and recovered his breath and composure. He opened his eyes and took a gulp of water.

"Right lads, let's be going." He moved towards the hole where the door had been just as another man came crashing through the space and almost fell into the same corner Michael had just vacated. He was covered in orange dust and had blood down one side of his uniform.

"George, thank the Lord, you're safe. Is that blood yours?" Michael moved hastily to his friend and knelt at his side.

"No mate, it's not mine. Some poor bugger back there. He told me he worked in a small shop before this show. He said he liked riding his bike around the village delivering groceries. He asked me if his mother would be pleased with him. Those were his last words. Poor blighter copped one in the neck."

"There's no glory here, is there?" Michael spoke quietly for George's ears alone.

"I hope those at home don't know the truth of all this. It's for them we're doing it. Remember that. We'll go back to smiling eyes and warm arms, you see if we don't. That'll be our glory."

This is one good bloke, Michael thought. *Thank God for friends like him. I couldn't manage without him. I want us both to make it out alive.*

CHAPTER 24

Delphi sat on her bunk and wrote to Rose.

July 1916
Dearest Rose,

Here I am at a camp behind the lines. I cannot tell you exactly where, but there has been a tremendous battle not too far from here. We hear the guns all the time and stories that make you cold to think about. How our chaps are coping, I do not understand.

I was given a promotion just after we arrived and so I am no longer peeling vegetables but doing a lot of paperwork concerning quantities and orders needed. I thought I would try and devise some new recipes too, but I'm not sure whether they will be well received by the 'powers that be'. It is quite a challenge but hopefully worth it. When I see the faces of the boys as they collect the food we have provided, I know we are helping to win this war. Sometimes they arrive so grey and haggard, but after a day or two of rest and good food they are ready to take up the fight again. Am I getting them back up just to fall again and even be killed? That's my guilt at the moment.

I also have anxiety that we are relieving men from the duties I am doing here so they can go and fight. If they are not here preparing food, they must go to the front. Am I condemning them by being here and doing their work?

She paused. *Shall I reveal my secret?* she thought. *Why not?*

Wonder of wonders. I have seen George three times recently. He borrowed a bicycle and rode over. It was only a fleeting meeting each time, but it has confirmed what I suspected from all our letters. Rose, I do believe I love him, and he loves me. What will the censor think of that! There are many who come here from our area at home, so I live in hope of seeing him again before they must move on. Now I know they are not too far away, maybe he can visit again, or they may even take their stand-down here.

Life in this camp can be quite jolly with the other girls, but you would not believe the conditions in which I am living. You would be very proud of me if you saw the plainness of it all. Around us the woods are full of greenery, though, and they remind me there is still beauty to be had. Hark at me! Would you consider your worldly sister could be so prosaic?

Please give my love to Mama and Papa. I will write to them tomorrow. Right now, I have work to do, so no more.

Much love, dearest Rose,

From your hardworking sister Delphi XX

"Did you say the 19th Manchesters?" Delphi quizzed the girl who had come to her office to deliver some receipts.

"Yes, they'll be here for two days' rest before heading back up the line, so I've also brought the numbers for their meals during that time."

"Right. Right, thank you," Delphi answered. She felt disoriented and distracted all of a sudden and sat back in her chair.

"Are you all right, ma'am?" The young girl stood in front of her desk with a slight frown.

"Mmm? Yes, sorry, Withers. I'll get onto this straight away. Dismissed."

"Yes, ma'am." The girl turned and headed for the door to return to the cook house.

Delphi stared ahead, unseeing, for several moments before urgency reclaimed her.

Despite the mountain of work on her desk, her mind kept wandering. Would she see George again? What of Michael? She and he had both grown up significantly since they'd last met. That must be true. If she saw him again now, she would not feel the same as when she had flung herself immodestly at him. She was sure of that.

Her imagination returned to images of George. His quirky smile, his unfashionable hair, his eyes that seemed to penetrate her soul.

We cannot plan our feelings. I know that now. I could not make Michael love me, but George and I seem to have an unspoken understanding, she thought. *I believe in destiny. I was not intended for Michael Redfern. I was meant to wait for George to appear in my life.*

Days passed.

"What in thunder is that noise?" Delphi sprang up, addressing her companion who had been gently snoring in the next bed. Edna had shared her billet for a while now, and they knew each other's hopes and dreams.

"I bet it's the moment you've been waiting for. Let's hope Lover Boy is with them." She spoke with her eyes still closed.

"He's not that … yet." Delphi laughed but crossed her fingers for several seconds.

Wrapping a shawl around her shoulders, she peered through the edge of the grubby window. Sure enough, two trucks were rumbling in, their engines making a racket. Filthy men swung from the rear of each one and several others were straggling along the track to the camp on foot. They looked exhausted, feet shuffling and heads hanging.

"Poor souls." Delphi looked to her friend. "They're covered in mud and look absolutely drained."

She turned back to the window, searching for anyone familiar. She scanned the morass of men for that freckled face; not that she would see the freckles under all that grime.

"You'd better get some clothes on quick, my lovely, if you want to find anyone," Edna said with a wicked grin and a sparkle in her eyes.

Delphi quickly braided her hair and thrust her long limbs into her uniform. She had managed a trickle of water optimistically called a bath the night before, although she hadn't hung around since it was so chilly and dispiriting.

By the time Delphi had reached the unloading area, most of the men had disappeared into the mess tent. As Administrator she had every right to access most areas, including that of the officers. White cloths covered the tables here and girls in aprons served breakfast. Eggs, fried bread and bacon with great mugs of tea to wash it down were handed around.

They ate with primitive pleasure. Delphi scanned the room as she stood just inside the doorway. She could see no one she recognised, and her eyes began to burn as she held back tears of frustration. She turned to leave with speed.

She spun with her head down to avoid anyone's gaze and immediately bumped into someone coming in. Thrown into confusion, she cried out, "Careful!"

"Delphi!"

She looked up to see George's eyes upon her. They shone from a face that was clean but for a streak of mud down one cheek.

She had imagined this moment so many times. She would be mopping his brow or supporting his weary frame as she sat him down and provided much-needed food. After, she would let him rest his head in her lap as he knelt before her. This meeting bore no reflection of those images, but was more precious for that.

Tears finally tumbled down Delphi's face.

"Delphi, my love," he said. "You will never know how pleased I am to find you here. It has been so long, too long." He took a step back, the better to look at her.

"George, I feared you were not in this contingent. I came to find you and you weren't here."

He took her elbow, guided her from the tent. She leaned into him.

"Aren't you hungry?"

"Not now," he answered. "Not for eggs and bacon, anyway." He smiled at her and she felt a flitter deep down inside.

He held her from him and looked intently at her. She raised her chin. He lowered his head and gently kissed her lips, which parted ever so slightly.

He murmured his contentment but managed to pull away before intensity struck. "Sorry about that. I couldn't help it. Michael will wonder where I've got to," he said. "I hoped you would still be here, but I didn't know for sure. This damn war is throwing up too many uncertainties."

"There's one thing of which I am certain," Delphi responded. "I'm certainly pleased to see you, dearest George. And there is nothing to be sorry for. Am I being too bold?"

"There is no time to dither these days, and when did you ever, anyway? It's part of why I love you."

She looked up at him with eyes wide.

"Who knows what might arrive upon us next? Come, we must return. Have you some moments to say hello to Michael before you get on with your work? He would like to greet you and ask after people at home, I know."

"Yes," she replied but quaked a little inside.

She knew she had made a complete fool of herself when she had offered Michael her love. It had not really bothered her the last time they'd met, when the four of them had visited the park. She had enjoyed flirting with both George and Michael in order to disconcert him. Life had been a game back then, before this war really got under way. Now she remembered her declaration with shame.

As they approached the mess tent, Delphi spotted Michael straight away. His height made him visible amongst those who were heading that way.

"Michael, over here, just coming," George called and waved.

Michael turned. "Delphi, it's wonderful to meet you again after so long."

"I'll leave you two to catch up for a few minutes," George said tactfully and headed in to get his food. "I'll see you in a minute, Michael. I'm starving."

Delphi turned to him to save her from further embarrassment, but he was already moving away. "Michael, that time when you were leaving … I made a fool of myself and I'm sorry for it," she said, looking at the ground.

"We were both young and experimenting with life. It seems such a long time ago. How are your family? I gather your mother is not coping with the loss of Hector."

"You were with him, weren't you?"

"Yes, I was. He was calm at the end. He had been enjoying army life. I don't understand that really, but he seemed to take great delight in the challenges and danger handed to him."

"Mother is in a sorry state," Delphi told him.

"I heard that from Rose."

"She still writes to you, then?" Delphi was surprised.

"Her letters mean such a lot to me," Michael confessed. "I imagine she sees quite a bit of Thom, though, both working in Manchester as they do."

He sighed and Delphi glanced up at him and wondered what he was thinking.

"I expect to hear at any time that they are engaged to be married," he said.

She noticed his eyes had a distant look, which set her wondering. "Not yet, as far as I know. I am sure she would have told me of any changes since we met last. I must go, Michael. I have a huge pile of work on my desk. What time is it?"

He dug in his pocket and pulled out his watch. "It's nearly ten o'clock."

"Is that a 'Fumsup Touch Wud' there on the chain?"

"Yes, it's my talisman. He's lost one eye, though. See?"

Delphi touched the tiny silver manikin. "Did someone give it to you?" Delphi wondered if he had a secret admirer.

"It belonged to Rose. She sent it to me in a package not long after my first real action. He has been with me constantly since then."

"I thought he looked familiar. At least he is keeping you safe," Delphi said, smiling up at him. "Rose will be pleased and very relieved."

"Do you think so?" There was hope in his tone.

CHAPTER 25

Delphi glanced behind her several times but everyone else seemed to be busy, and those in sight were not taking notice of her movements. It was not unusual for girls to take a break from the grey and brown of camp life by strolling in the woods to pick wildflowers. The difference was they did not usually go alone.

But then Delphi was not going to be alone for long. Her skin tingled. She smiled with secret anticipation.

Deeper and deeper into the wood she ventured. She stood still for a moment, listening. The birdsong was loud. It was dry and sunny, and had been for several days. The twin tones of a blue tit dominated, but there were others too. A blackbird on a topmost branch sang beautifully. It was probably a lone robin not far away that was twittering and chattering.

Sunbeams shot through the branches. She smiled now that she was alone. All the tension of her escape slipped away.

As she approached the spot, she saw him leaning against a tree, one leg bent behind him where his foot rested on the trunk. She stopped to delight in the sight of his beloved figure, so tall and straight.

I shouldn't be doing this, but I want to, I truly do, she thought. *He is brave and frightened, and I want to give him this gift. As he said, there isn't time to dither these days. It's not in my nature anyway.*

As she walked forward, she thought, *I shall remember this perfume until I'm an old lady, if I come through this war unscathed.*

George heard her and turned, smiling. Her heart flipped.

"I wasn't sure you would come," he said.

She moved towards him. "I needed to," she answered simply.

"Are you sure? I shall do nothing about which you are uneasy. Let's walk."

He took her hand and turning it gently he kissed the inside of her wrist and then her palm. He closed her fingers, sealing the kiss within. Her heart pitched yet again — nerves or excitement, she wasn't sure which. Turning, he clasped her other hand and they began to pick their way through the flowers, following a narrow path worn by some unseen animal there before them.

"You have no idea of the pleasure being here with you is giving me. It's all so clean and fresh, and these woods are vibrant with life. I dread going back. That's not brave, is it, Delphi?" He stopped walking and turned to her.

"I've seen the state you boys arrive here in. I've smelled the mud and observed the fright in the eyes of those before you. Sometimes when they hold out their plate to be served, their hands are trembling with distress. I watched the exhausted stagger as you arrived. To go back to something you fear is more than brave," she said.

After a short while, Delphi took off her hat and felt the warmth of the day upon her hair.

"Come through here." George bent to lead the way and she followed through a short tunnel made by the branches.

"Oh, it's like a little room. How amazing!" She looked about. "How did you know about this?"

"I came exploring while you worked yesterday afternoon."

The waxy leaves of the bushes swept thickly all around in a great swathe, but in the middle a space remained. It was covered with springy, bright green turf and the sun shone on the grass. Delphi tossed her hat down and turned to George, who encircled her in his strong embrace. His lips were firm as they found hers, which parted to welcome him. She laughed as he released her. She stepped away and reached up to unpin her hair, watching him all the while with dancing eyes.

"Don't play with me, Delphi."

"This is no game, George," she responded, suddenly serious. "I believe I've loved you since we first met, and all the while we have been writing I've become more and more in need of your love."

"You have my love, all of it."

Her long dark hair tumbled down and she dropped the pins into her hat. "I shall need those again before we leave. You see? I'm not playing. I am being practical. This is real and I'm ready, dearest George."

He took a step towards her and kissed her with much greater urgency, to which she firmly responded.

As they parted for a moment, Delphi said, "I'm not sure what to do. This is all new to me." She smiled, feeling demure and uncertain and shrinking a little into herself.

"We need do nothing more if you are unsure. It will be difficult for me, but I understand. We can wait until this damn war is over."

"George, I am yours. Life is uncertain at the moment, but of this I'm sure." She took his hand and guided it down her body, no longer needing to know what to do but feeling the naturalness of her actions.

His arms encircled her again, and with one knee to the ground he gently lowered her onto the grass. Slowly, watching him all the while, she began to undo the buttons of her uniform as she lay there breathing heavily.

They returned to reality from their shared ecstasy some while later.

"Heavens, what time is it? I must get back. I don't want the real world to come in yet, though," Delphi said, sitting up and turning to him. "Dearest George." She turned and kissed him gently.

They helped each other dress quickly, and Delphi held her pins in her mouth as she rewound her hair.

"Will I do? Do I look different? I feel utterly changed. I'm sure people will notice." She laughed.

"You still look delectable, my Delphi." He took her face in his hands and kissed her forehead.

They returned through the woods but before they emerged, he drew her close one last time.

"Delphi, we must be married. This situation is not right. It doesn't fit with my views on things at all. I don't need permission from my Commander, but maybe we should gather the right paperwork and approach a minister to marry us as soon as possible. It will mean you must return to England, but I should be happier with your safety secured too."

She looked up at him.

"I'm asking you to marry me as soon as it can be arranged, my love."

"And my answer is yes, George. I will marry you."

"We only have tomorrow morning and then I have to be gone. Duty calls, but I think it could be managed within the next month. Please wait for me."

Delphi gasped, grabbing his tunic. "Of course I shall."

He brushed a strand of hair from her face with gentle fingers. "Wait here while I return to the camp first. I shall not leave you with idle talk to contend with. God bless you, darling Delphi."

"But I must see you before you leave." She was sounding desperate.

"You shall. We'll meet before I go, but it must be brief. We shall not have the time to come this way again, my dearest. Not this leave, but maybe I shall get through again soon. I love you. I love you."

"Look after him, Michael," Delphi said in desperation after she had watched George climb onto the back of the truck the following morning. She was aware of his eyes on her, but he'd refused to embrace her in public, not wanting to leave her to the gossips after he left.

Michael held up his little Fumsup Touch Wud figure. "We shall be fine, Delphi," he said and gave her a reassuring smile. "Tell Rose when you write that I think of her often. Even if her heart lies with Thom, her letters hearten me and her little gift is with me always."

Delphi smiled through her tears. She was determined that George would remember her smile as he went, but it was proving very difficult.

She watched as the trucks disappeared around a bend in the rutted roadway. Then she turned and ran.

She banged the door behind her and flung herself into the chair at her desk. The tears could fall at last. Her cheeks ached and her eyes stung from holding in her grief and she sobbed. Not quiet, beautiful sobs but heart-wrenching gulps of sorrow which left her face red and swollen.

Edna found her a short time later. "Come here, dearest," she said as she came around the desk and held Delphi to her chest. Delphi continued to heave, but her tears had dried at last.

"I didn't know it was possible to feel this way about someone else. Half of me is wrenched away and I have no knowledge of when it will return. That's the worst of it. What if…"

"Shh," soothed Edna. "We'll have no 'what ifs' here. Think about the time you had together while he was here and be joyful for that."

CHAPTER 26

"Rose, you look so tired," Izzy said. "Do you have to work like this?"

"Yes, dearest, I must."

"There must be more and more relatives visiting to find out what has happened to their husband, father, son, brother."

Rose smiled at her youngest sister and said nothing of all the men who simply disappeared. "Dear Izzy," she said and gave her a hug.

"I wish I could do something to help our boys like you do."

"You do help. You help a great deal with all the knitting, baking and packing that you do. That is such valuable work. I know from the letters I get from Michael that he and his men really appreciate the parcels they receive."

"Do you still write to him?"

"Yes, I do. It seems to help somehow."

"Perhaps Michael will take up with you when he returns."

"No, of course not, you silly-dilly," Rose said with a forced smile. "Michael is only a friend. His heart lies elsewhere, I believe. Although I think that is not going to fulfil itself. Now, I must get on, and you have your piano practice." She took Izzy's face between her hands and lightly kissed the top of her head.

"Well, maybe you should reconsider Thom, then. You need to consider marrying someone."

That evening Rose took off her hat and was unbuttoning her coat as her eyes strayed to the salver. There was a letter. The envelope was small, and the paper was thin with a franking mark in the corner that she recognised. Her heart bounded and her calm evaporated.

Flinging her coat on the chair with uncharacteristic carelessness, she snatched up the letter and ran upstairs to her room. Closing the door, she sat on her bed, ripping open the envelope.

July 1916
My dearest Rose,

I carried your Fumsup with me into the worst battle we have faced so far. I imagine you will already know of the high casualties that we have suffered because of the work that you do, but I am unscathed. I have lost many good men and some friends. My battalion was lucky. We had the French on one side of us and their knowledge of the bombardment required before we went over the top was invaluable. Others did not fare so well, and many thousands have been killed. Thousands, my dear Rose! I cannot describe nor would I wish you to know what it was like.

Thank goodness I have such a good friend in George Dight. We keep each other sane in this insanity. He has a deep faith with which he does not shower me, but it seems to make him calm in the heat of the madness around us. He has a great sense of humour, too, and seems to find humanity in the unlikeliest of places, which keeps things in perspective for us both.

My little talisman has lost an eye, I am sorry to say, and he has a dent in one side, but he and I are muddling through together. He reminds me of your calm grey eyes, thoughts of which also bring me sanity in those short moments of peace which we value so much.

Rose stopped reading for a moment. A smile spread across her face. Those calm grey eyes were not calm at that moment but shining with joy at his words. Then her hopes were dashed yet again as she resumed her reading.

The other news I have is that we had a few days' rest behind the lines and we met Delphi. She seems well and is her usual lovely and happy self. She and George seem to have hit it off in a big way, as I dare say you already know. She was a welcome sight: a bright flower among all the muck and mud. We were sorry to say goodbye, all of us.

Dearest Rose, I think of you often. I hope you think kindly of me.

My very best wishes,

Michael

Rose sat for many minutes. Then she stood slowly, folded the letter and placed it in her drawer with the others and the meagre treasures she had kept. She spotted the handkerchief Michael had given her all those years ago when life was less complicated, and dreams were still alive. She raised it to her cheek in contemplation. Then she fingered the little pink rose in the corner. Bought with thoughtfulness, she'd hoped, by Michael — but she had come to believe it had probably been chosen by his mother.

Later that evening she sat at her desk and wrote.

My dear Thom,

I have been thinking long and hard about the times we have spent together and I realise that you are a good friend: true, trustworthy and loyal. We have fun and laugh with each other, and you are kind and considerate. I know I said that I could not see our long-term future together, but I am beginning to think…

Just as she reached this point, there was a shout and crash from the landing, followed by moans. Rose flung down her pen, pushed back her chair and hurried to the door. By the time she had it open and rushed out, there was pandemonium at the foot of the wide staircase and lying at the bottom was her mother. "Mama!" she shouted.

Mr Strong had emerged from his study and Dora came waddling along the passage from the kitchen as fast as her stout legs would carry her.

"Oh, Mama!" Izzy shouted as she followed Rose down the stairs.

Rose knelt with her father, who had already removed his jacket and covered his wife's torso. "I shall fetch the doctor immediately," she said, standing and turning to Dora. "Please fetch my coat and hat, and Izzy's too. Izzy, you must come with me."

"But I don't want to leave Mama," wailed her sister. Rose could see she would be better with an occupation.

"I need you, Izzy. Come, Papa will look after Mama."

They returned in Doctor Master's motor car. By the time they got indoors, Mrs Strong was sitting up. With the doctor's help and with Mr Strong's support on the other side, she managed to get to the sitting room. It transpired she had tripped on the stairs and had a concussion.

"You are extremely lucky, my dear," Mr Strong said.

"It might be better if that had been the end of me. This awful ache I still feel about Hector would be finished and you would all be relieved of my misery."

"It could so easily have been worse. What would I do without you if something were to happen? I miss Hector too, but we all love and need you as well. Surely the girls deserve your love too."

Mrs Strong remained quiet but thoughtful as she lay back on the pillows of the chaise longue. Thoughts of the unfinished letter on Rose's desk were gone for the time being as she knelt beside her mother.

CHAPTER 27

When Rose returned from a hasty lunch, there was a fresh batch of files on her desk. It was relentless, the endless stream of death and maiming. How did those in the trenches cope with it all, never mind the disease, mud and stench of human suffering?

She sighed and opened the first folder. At first it was just one more name; one more lad for whom she had to sort out the pay that was owed to his family. As she worked in Manchester, lots of the boys she had to deal with were local, but she had never known any of them. There were many City Battalions, and most had served in France in some of the bloodiest battles so far. An Australian this time, but he'd been serving with the British armed forces. She read the name: Dight, George Arthur.

"Oh Lord!" She sat back in her chair. Surely not! She looked again and reread the name and then the regiment. The 19th Manchesters, it detailed, killed at Flers in northern France and buried in a temporary grave as most of them were. Died of wounds, it said.

Has Delphi heard? This was her first thought. Probably not. Why would she? She was unrelated. Just a friend. Did Michael know? He must do. They served together. Why had she not heard from him about it? Oh! Oh no! Had he been wounded or worse, killed in the same battle?

She reached for the rest of the folders and as if a mania had overtaken her, she opened each one, reading the first names. Nothing.

Relief threatened to swamp her. Then she slumped. Maybe the file just hadn't arrived yet. Perhaps it was sitting on the desk of one of the other girls.

As she leaped up, her chair skidded back and hit the wall. Ignoring it, she rushed into the next room where the pool of others worked. Trying to restrain the urgency in her voice, she composed her face and pulled rank to make her request.

"If you come across a folder for Lieutenant Michael Redfern, please inform me immediately. It's very important. In fact, perhaps you would do a quick scan of pending files now."

She retreated to her own little office and slowly got out the forms she needed to make ready for George's family. Maybe even they had not received the news yet. Australia was such a long way for news to travel, and she didn't know whether they lived in a town or miles from anywhere.

Before she left for the train that afternoon, she delayed as long as possible just in case there was a message from the room next door about Michael, but nothing arrived.

When Rose came home that evening, her eyes automatically sought out the salver on the hall table. Her heart bumped as she saw a letter, the size and colour of which she recognised immediately.

She hurried across without taking off her hat and coat and snatched it up. She did not even wait to take it to her room but ripped it open and read its contents with greed.

Dearest Rose,

I imagine you have not heard that our friend and my best companion has been killed. I still cannot believe it but for the giant hole that has been left in my mind. He and I had become close comrades as only men in our circumstances can be. We relied upon each other to keep our spirits up and I miss him most dreadfully.

I saw him fall. I dropped my weapon and ran to him. Rose, he was in my arms when he died. It was horrible. I am lost, so bereft do I feel. I keep seeing it all replaying in my head, over and over again. I am so tired.

I have tried to sleep since I wrote the last paragraph. I must carry on for all of you at home, but it is hard. My heart is no longer in it.

I don't know what effect this will have on your sister. It will be hard, and I wonder how she will cope away from you as she serves her country in France.

My other news is that I will be coming home for a few days of extra training. It would be so good if I could be sent to Manchester. I cannot believe my good fortune with this and it cannot come too soon. I am finding this intolerable just at this time. I find I cannot bear the interminable noise, smell and close confines of so many men. I feel impervious to the danger and that makes me most vulnerable. I need to survive long enough to make this leave.

I have your little Fumsup with me, and I touch his tiny wooden head for luck frequently. He reminds me of home and of you, Rose. Thank you.

I believe I shall see you soon.

Best wishes to you and your family and I hope you might be able to help Delphi too, in some way.

Your good friend,
Michael

At this point Rose struggled out of her coat and hat while clutching the precious letter. She ran up the stairs to the sanctuary of her room.

That evening Rose sat at her dressing table. The unfinished letter to Thom was still there, pushed to one side. She tore it in half. She could not contemplate that just now. She started a much more difficult message.

Dearest Delphi,

How do I tell you this in a letter? I want you here with me so that I might hold you close. I know you and George have become good friends.

Rose decided she probably did not know the half of it, but she gathered her sister had become very close to George. These were difficult times for everyone, and Delphi had a mercurial temperament. Rose knew this was going to be devastating.

Through the work that I do, I had some very distressing news today...

CHAPTER 28

Delphi heaved into the bucket and then wiped her mouth.

"Bad enough that I have to smell those greens cooking without having a sick bug as well," she shouted out to Edna, who had followed her across the yard to the latrine area. "Having to come in here doesn't help either," she added.

As she emerged, her friend looked at her. "I think those boys who came in the other day must have brought it with them. People are going down with it all over the place. Please don't give it to me."

"At least I have to stay away from the kitchens for the time being. It's the smell of the bully beef cooking that is the worst."

"Mind you, there are all manner of smells around here that would set off the staunchest stomach," Edna added.

"Ooh, don't," Delphi groaned and headed back to the latrine. When she was finally done, she staggered out looking pale and sweaty.

"You poor old dear. Give me your arm and we'll put you to bed. You seem to have a really bad bout. It's lasting a bit longer than for other people."

They entered the billet and Delphi collapsed onto her bunk.

"Postman's been," Edna said, waving a letter. "Looks like your sister's writing," she added. "Not from Lover Boy, I'm afraid."

"Leave it there. I'll read it later," Delphi muttered with her eyes closed. "I'm concentrating on not being sick again."

"Well, I'll go now and give you some quiet. I better get on. There's a lot to do with all you people being ill."

"Sorry."

"You might be soon, when you have to cover my shift. Sleep tight."

Delphi slept fitfully for the next hour and a half. When she awoke, she felt considerably better. She got up and ambled across for the correspondence from Rose, pulling the paper from the envelope as she returned to sit on her bed. She read what her sister had written. She sat in silence for several minutes then rose and left the hut. She clutched the letter in a fist that crumpled the paper and stepped with care across the yard, around the corner and through the woods. She found the little path with ease, and stooping through the tunnel of branches she lowered herself to the ground, hugged her knees and put her head down. There was no wailing, no sobbing, no flinging herself about.

Rose would be surprised at me. No, perhaps she wouldn't. Rose would understand completely, she thought.

Still she clutched the letter. Later, very slowly she unfurled the crumpled paper and reread what her sister had told her.

Dearest Delphi,

How do I tell you this in a letter? I want you here with me so that I might hold you close. I know you and George have become good friends.

Through the work that I do, I had some very distressing news today. George Dight has been killed. I cannot dress it up for you. He died of wounds at a place called Flers in the Somme and he has a temporary grave there. Darling sister, I am so, so sorry and wish I could be with you to hold you tight and keep you safe from anguish. I have a notion you were closer to him than any of us knew.

Try not to despair, Delphi. Keep him close in your heart and replay the times you shared and the memories you have made. Come home if you need to.

Your loving sister,
Rose

Eventually Delphi got up. She was cold and her joints felt stiff. After brushing down her skirt, she shook her head. Grief must wait.

I shall deal with this later. It might be an error. These things happen all the time. There are mix-ups and people go missing in the confusion and then reappear. This is not official, she told herself.

That evening, back at work in her office, there was a rap at the door and Edna came in.

"It's well past knocking off time, Delphi. You're working too hard, especially since you've been ill for several days on and off. Surely you need to eat something, even if it's just a light snack. Apart from anything else it will help you gather strength to fight your grief, my dear. You left your sister's letter on your bed when you came over here. I know you are suffering, despite the fact you've said nothing."

Delphi did her best to ignore Edna's last comment. "This sick bug is certainly hanging on. Most of the others only had it for a couple of days." She slumped back in her chair. Then her mood changed. She thumped her fist down on the desk. "Why us, Edna? Why did he have to go and get himself killed? I didn't want him to be a hero or anything. He should have kept his head down."

"This anger is all part of the process of getting awful news. Grief takes many forms and you must work through it. The real sadness will follow, and you need to accept the help from those who are able to give it," Edna said.

Delphi put her hands to her face and covered her eyes.

"Come with me. Let's go to the canteen for something to eat. You must be hungry again by now."

"It won't help. It won't help at all," Delphi answered, her voice rising. "Why did he have to be so careless? Plenty of others are surviving. It's just not fair. He was one of God's few. Why did He abandon him?" She put her head in her hands.

"You're trying to manage all this on your own. I really think you should go and see Controller Swaine and ask for a spell at home. Your family will be there to help you."

"No, I can't do that. Plenty of other people have things to cope with. For goodness' sake, Edna. I can't run away. No, I need to get on with my work. I can't simply disappear at the first sign of trouble. Come on, you're right. Let's go and eat." Delphi tossed her head and stood. She grabbed her hat and rammed it on.

A few days later, there was a message for Delphi to go to Controller Swaine's office.

"What now? I've got a mountain of things to do," she said to Edna.

"Only one way to find out," her friend answered.

"Miss Strong," the Controller said, "it has come to my attention that you have been unwell and are finding it more difficult than others to throw off this sickness. Is there any reason for this that you can think of?"

"No, ma'am, not at all." Under no circumstances was Delphi going to share what she suspected. Time would tell, and she would deal with that when she was certain.

"I'm going to give you a Blighty…"

"Oh, but…"

"Excuse me, Administrator Strong." The officer before her spoke in an authoritative tone.

"Ma'am," Delphi said meekly. She would rail against it when she returned to Edna.

"You are clearly rundown and overtired. We need fit and healthy girls here. You have excelled in your work so far, so this is a reward that others will not receive. So be grateful for that and take it." She smiled broadly in a way that Delphi had never seen before. "That will be all."

When she returned to her billet, Edna was there. Her eyes were like organ stops as Delphi recounted her meeting with the Controller.

"Grab it and run," Edna declared.

Just before she left, as she and Edna neared the canteen, Delphi remembered when she'd bumped into George in the doorway. She tried to capture his face in her mind and found a myriad of other images blocked it out. She hesitated. Edna turned to see her face contort.

"What if I forget what he looks like? What if I can't remember his voice with its funny accent? Edna, I'm scared."

"Your sister is an artist, is she not?"

Delphi looked puzzled for a moment. "You mean I could ask her to paint his image for me? Yes, she could do that with ease, I am sure."

"That way, you will have an easy reminder always."

"Maybe there will be other ways he will always be with me," she said to herself and moved forward with greater assurance.

CHAPTER 29

When Delphi arrived home, her family greeted her with ecstatic delight.

"My darling, we are so proud of you," Mrs Strong said.

Delphi noted the effort with which Mama was trying to take part in household affairs. Rose placed her arm around her mother's shoulders and Izzy ran forward to give her returning sister a hug.

"It's lovely to see you, Delphi," she said.

"You look a little peaky, my dear," said her father.

"It's been a long journey, Papa."

"Tell us all about your adventure," her mother said. "Thank goodness it's over and you're safe with us again."

"I do hope to return, Mama," Delphi answered.

"Well, yes, of course. Let's not think of that, though. You have only just returned. Dora will unpack your things later."

"Before you come down for dinner, you must have a rest," her Papa added.

Delphi gave a tight smile and retired to her room. As she leaned against the inside of the bedroom door she had closed, she breathed deeply with appreciation for the solitude this space gave her. Eventually, she moved to sit motionless on the edge of the bed. Trying to act normally was a strain.

It wasn't long before a quiet knock sounded.

"Come in. Rose, is that you?"

Her older sister's face appeared around the door. "I can come back later, if you like."

"No, come in, please do."

"You look so weary, Delphi. I see you are sorrowful, but there is something more, I think. Is there anything you want to share with me? It will go no further until you are ready, I promise."

"Oh, Rose, you know me too well." Delphi smiled, but it was wan and half-hearted.

"Are you planning to go back?"

"I doubt it," Delphi answered. "I needed to throw Mama off the scent, as it were."

Rose put her head on one side and raised her eyebrows. "Is there something to keep you here?"

"You know, don't you, Rose? You've guessed the cause of my shame."

"When your sickness continued beyond the normal time of such an infection, as you wrote, yes, I think I guessed correctly, didn't I?"

"What am I to do? I dare not tell Mama and Papa. I shall be disgraced. There will be a huge scandal for the whole family. Your chances and those for Izzy to find a husband will be affected. I'm so sorry. George is not here to protect me. We would have married. He asked me. We had it all planned." She lowered her head and pulled at the fabric of her skirt, folding it and creasing it over and over.

"I know it, Delphi, I do."

"You can tell me I am selfish and foolish. I know all that to be true. Say what you must be thinking, that I am vile and dishonourable, contemptible even."

"Hush, Delphi. You are none of those things. You loved a man to distraction and the two of you have been in the most abominable situation about which I can only guess. Who am I to be judgemental?"

"Ha! Plenty of people will swoop into your place and have their say. Of that you may be certain."

"We shall need to be practical. When is the baby due?"

Delphi smiled without mirth. "Rose, always so pragmatic."

"And possibly sensible, Delphi dear, but hopefully not hard-headed or unsentimental."

"Sorry, I didn't mean to be insulting. You are the kindest, wisest, strongest person I know. I am so grateful to have you as my sister."

"Steady on there." Rose smiled. "I'm not always wise in my own affairs, I can assure you, but that's a story for another time. So, tell me, when is it due?"

They discussed dates.

"So, we need do nothing just yet. No one else need hear of this for a while until we have decided the best plan. We shall keep all information between us and talk more in a day or two when you are rested," Rose said and gave her sister a hug.

As she left the room, closing the door silently, Rose sighed and wondered how on earth to get around this problem. In no way was she as optimistic as she had tried to appear for Delphi's benefit.

The next morning Rose walked with her sister. For once the gardens held no distraction.

"I wrote to Mr and Mrs Dight in Australia as soon as I had the news of George's passing, Delphi. That is part of my work, contacting relatives."

"Yes, I believe you said." Delphi spoke with uncharacteristic restraint and her head hung down.

"Well, I received a reply. It was addressed to me personally, although it came to my office. They are coming all the way to England to collect his things and are due to arrive in about four weeks. They're sailing on a troop ship with the Adelaide Steamship Company from Fremantle. It's in Western Australia, apparently. The journey takes six and a half weeks in total and is due to reach Plymouth only about a month from now."

"I suppose they'll go to London; I should think they'll need to visit the War Office first," Rose murmured. "Are they going to contact us when they have concluded their business? I wonder what they are like. Oh, Rose, will this feeling ever lessen? I cannot believe I shall not see George again. I'm frightened I'll forget him; the sound of his voice." Tears welled again in her lovely eyes. "I have his photograph, the one I showed you, but it's so formal in his uniform and just grey and white. It has none of his vitality and life."

That final word was her undoing. The silent tears turned to heart-breaking sobs. Rose enfolded her sister and felt her own eyes well. She held Delphi until the waterfall subsided and Delphi was left weary and sad. With arms around each other, they made their way to the little shelter at the end of the lavender walk.

"I have been cruel to you in the past, Rose," Delphi said, "and you have been nothing but loyal and loving. I need to tell you."

"No, you don't, Delphi. You have no need to say anything. You are my sister, warts and all!" She smiled. "We were young, and things were different."

Rose looked up at the wisteria branches that edged the roof of the little shelter. They had grown and thickened considerably in the intervening years. How changed they all were. Hector killed, Mama wasting away but putting on a brave face, so many boys gone and those who returned altered by the horrors they'd endured. Delphi's life would never be the same.

And herself? Well, she might be single forever because of the loyalty she had to one man.

"Would you like me to paint a small portrait of him from the photograph? If you don't like it or it's not good enough, you need not keep it."

"I should like that greatly, Rose. Thank you."

"I didn't know him well, but I think I can get the sunlight shining on the strands of his hair and the spark in his eyes."

"Oh, Rose…"

"Now…" She paused. "The thing is, Delphi, George's parents have asked if they could come and meet us. You must know George wrote to them about you and they are keen to see you in particular. His mother sounds sympathetic and friendly. She didn't seem formal or stuffy at all."

"How can I cope with that?" Delphi wiped her eyes. "What will they say about me and this mess I have got myself into? I couldn't bear it if they were horrid. I don't want anything to spoil my memories. Nor do I want George's child blighted by harsh talk."

"I do feel they won't," Rose said, as the germ of an idea took root in her mind.

CHAPTER 30

Dear Rose,

Rose read the appellation and sighed. *Sometimes it's 'dearest', other times 'my dearest' and this time just 'dear'. I don't know what to think. Now that George is gone, is he thinking of Delphi again? My affections for him are constant, but I lurch from one place to another when wondering if I stand any chance at all. It would seem not, yet still he writes,* she thought.

She carried on reading.

I cannot believe this good fortune that I am being sent back to Blighty for special training and will be coming close to home. It will not be for long, but I shall arrive in a couple of weeks. I cannot wait to escape from this place. Being with all these men together in confinement is like living in a boarding dormitory or a prison. I am so weary of the snoring, scratching and worse each night. Oh, for a little solitude with birdsong and bubbling water.

I hope we might meet. I could buy you a hot chocolate and we could walk beside the river. We could smell the mown grass and appreciate all the colours of which you write.

My dear Rose, I fear I will be greatly changed in your eyes, but perhaps you will afford me the luxury of your company for a short while. That would help me immensely.

Your humble friend,
Michael

Rose stared at the paper in her hand and then realised its fineness was wafting in the breeze and her unsteady hand was not helping. She reread the last sentences, trying to make sense of her emotions.

Just then the door burst open, startling Rose from her reverie. Izzy was waving a letter and looking amazed.

"You'll never guess what! Frau Schröder wrote to me. She managed to get to Switzerland in the end."

"Who?"

"Frau Schröder, my German teacher. Wake up, Rose, whatever is the matter? She writes about the Judenzählung: it's a census of all Jews in Germany. It proves that eighty per cent *have* been fighting — for Germany, I'm afraid, but that's where they live. The propaganda denies that and is trying to say that they are lacking in patriotism."

"Why is this of interest to you, dearest?"

"Well, it's not their fault they happened to end up in the wrong country. They have no homeland. It's just another example of German lies and aggression, isn't it?"

"I see," Rose said, only half listening.

"Ever since those riots two or three years ago, I've been interested in the Jewish question. They have a very rough deal much of the time."

"I suppose they do. Where did you say Frau Schröder is now? I know she went to the American Embassy when she left here."

"There was the possibility of her being found work as a cook, but the grant the Americans were offering was too tiny for her to continue working here. Not good to be German here now, of course. Gisela told me she is finding it difficult with the name calling. Then they talked of repatriation for Frau Schröder. I told you before. Fancy being in Switzerland. That's why she is able to write, albeit infrequently. She says after the war I could visit her. That would be such a good experience."

"Yes, it would. I'm pleased you and Gisela are good friends. She will be needing that. Oh dear, I don't know how I missed poor Frau Schröder's difficulties," Rose said.

"You've been so busy, Rose, and working such long hours," Izzy answered.

"Yes, I suppose so."

Izzy came to Rose's side and put her arm around her. "You do seem despondent, Rose. I suppose you are just overtired."

"Yes, that must be it, Izzy," Rose said and glanced at the letter in her hand.

The days seemed interminable. Rose was still busy, but her eyes wandered to the clock on the wall several times during each work session. She found herself staring at the dust motes as they swirled in the rays of sunlight that struck the window, too high to look out of.

Like the classrooms at school, Rose thought. *Designed to limit daydreaming and inattention.*

"I feel as if the whole of life is a waiting game, sometimes," she said to a colleague.

"I know. One of the things needed most is patience. Anyone who has an abundance of that will be fine."

I wonder when he will arrive. Perhaps he is here already. Maybe he'll change his mind and not get in touch at all. He might simply be getting in touch with me in order to see Delphi. No, in truth, I do not believe that of him. He would not be callous and use me in that way, of that I am sure. He would write directly to her with some excuse to meet.

She let herself into the hall each evening and her eyes could not help but stray to the salver where post and invitations were left. Not that there were many of the latter these days. Mama usually declined, and people had become reluctant to ask. Papa spent lots of evenings at his club after work. Rose was always at work and Izzy, well, Izzy occupied herself. She had her piano, she read, and she still sewed and knitted for the troops abroad.

The question of what to do about Delphi played on Rose's mind. Her parents were still in blissful ignorance of the pending conversation about her condition and where she might go for a confinement. On top of all this, Rose could not turn her mind away from Michael. She remembered all those years back when he'd received the cut to his temple fighting with the local boys and how she'd guided him to her home. She recalled the closeness of his muscular arms and chest and even the smell of him. No, not that, but the feelings it had stirred deep within her that she still felt to this day.

Please let him get in touch soon. It was so long since they had last met. What if he had changed? What if he was not the man he had been? What if…?

Day after day passed until finally, she opened the front door and there on the salver was a small envelope with writing she instantly recognised. The stamp was local.

He had written from Manchester. He was here. He was around the corner from where she worked. How could she not have felt his presence? He was living at home during his training. How had she not known which train or omnibus he caught each evening? How long had he been here?

She snatched up the card and in her haste promptly dropped it to the floor, where it skated across the polished wood and slid under the table. She was on her hands and knees to retrieve it when footsteps on the stairs above her head caused her to grab it and leap up as quickly as her long skirts and jacket would allow.

"What on earth are you doing, Rose?" Delphi stood at the bottom with one hand on the balustrade and a small frown puckering her brow. Her blue dress suited her, and her smooth complexion looked glowing now that she had stopped being ill each morning.

"I dropped something, that is all," Rose said. She didn't want to confess to Delphi that she had an invitation. "It's a bit dusty under there. Poor Dora is clearly struggling these days and Mama hasn't noticed," she said as a diversion. "You might help out a little, Delphi." She heard her voice growing irritable. "Especially with George's parents arriving before long. You want them to think well of us. I'm working long hours and you're doing nothing."

"Yes, Rose, you are right, of course," Delphi said, looking at the floor.

CHAPTER 31

Three days Rose had to wait, but now Saturday dawned bright and clear. It could not be better. The path to the park was familiar. Elderberries hung among the foliage that drooped over the fence next to the footpath. The leaves on the plane trees that lined the road were larger now than a couple of months ago, and the fruit started to form in blobs of furry green. Colours were darker. All was opulent, crammed, overflowing.

Rose hurried. She almost ran but managed to restrain herself. The lilac feather in her hat bobbed in time with her steps. It matched the trim of her neat little short coat. Her slim figure was accentuated by the cut of that cream-coloured jacket with its peplum and the skirt that was fuller than high fashion recommended. She had imagined herself in this outfit for such a long time. Now, having dressed with care, she was heading to meet him at last. Michael, her childhood love. Not that he knew it or would ever know it.

Rose's wayward hair exasperated her constantly. However, others saw how it framed her small face and smiled when they passed because she looked radiant and behind her spectacles her eyes sparkled with vitality. While Rose was aware of her shortcomings, nobody else noticed any at all on that vibrant Saturday morning.

She met friends of the family on her way.

Oh no. Can I avoid them? I don't want to be held up and have to say where I'm going, she thought with exasperation.

"Good day, Miss Strong. Lovely morning. How is your mother? I haven't seen her in such a while."

"Good morning, Mrs White, Mr White. She is well but very tired, I'm afraid."

"Such a beautiful day for a stroll," the gentleman said.

"Yes, indeed," Rose replied. *Come on, let me go*, she thought.

"We mustn't keep you," Mrs White said. "You seem in a hurry."

She's hoping to be informed of my mission, Rose thought. "Enjoy your morning." She bobbed her head and turned to leave.

Through the gates of the park she slowed to a more sedate pace.

And there he was.

He was half turned from her and looking up to the blue sky, so he did not notice her arrival. She stopped, suddenly breathless. Her heart thumped. Surely he would hear it from there. Maybe he did, for at that moment he faced her.

The sun caught each strand of his fair hair, slightly longer than when he had left for France the last time. His uniform emphasised the broadness of his shoulders and the length of his legs, or perhaps he was stronger and taller. He turned to her and raised his hand. He smiled. Her heart sang out across the intervening space and she knew beyond all doubt it was him or no one.

"Rose!" He strode towards her and with very few steps he was in front, towering over her. He clasped her fingers and held them just a little longer than protocol allowed.

"Michael, how lovely this is." She thought her pleasure would outshine the sun. She was not able to be coquettish. Her smile was one of complete joy and was the most natural of expressions.

"I cannot believe this is real," he said and turned to walk beside her. "Rose, your letters have kept me sane. You have no idea of the truth of that."

She didn't know what to say. He seemed to be walking closer to her side than was usual and he kept looking down at her. She was shy and insecure all at once.

Whether he guessed this or not she was unsure, but he said, "Let's go and sit for a while and have a cup of hot chocolate. There is so much news to catch up on. Maybe we need time to get used to each other's company again."

"Yes," was all she could answer.

The chocolate came, steaming and comforting. It wasn't long before they were chatting as of old.

"May we walk along the river? I've dreamed about that for so long," he said.

The river was full, but the bank was hard with a pathway worn into the grass. The water gurgled its way across the stones with a small backwash as it descended over a steeper incline, and then seemed to rest in the shadows of the willows that washed their wispy fingers at its edge. There were a few people further along the path but nobody to interrupt their passage.

"Let me just stand for a minute," Michael said and came to a halt and closed his eyes.

Rose stood silently at his side. She understood his need of the moment, but she took the opportunity to study his face.

His features were more angular. Perhaps he had lost weight. The stubble on his chin, though not long, caught the sun, as did his hair. The scar earned so many years ago was just visible amongst his forelock that still fell forwards in an unruly tumble. She was pleased his hair had been allowed to grow while he had spent long weeks in the warzone.

Taking a deep breath, he opened his eyes and looked at her with the full force of their blueness. "You are astonishing, Rose. Few women I have known would remain as calm and tranquil as you. You have an inner peace and grace. I need such grace to find my own again." He hung his head.

She simply smiled and shrugged imperceptibly. *I wonder how many women he has known*, she thought in her insecurity, focusing on this small thing rather than the compliment and hope he had just given her.

In that uncanny way of people who are close friends, he said, "I have known few women." He shrugged and smiled.

Her heart jumped as they started to stroll.

"I knew two sisters at a café in France, but they were very closely guarded by their father." He smiled. "One or two others I have met casually. Delphi, of course."

Rose took a sharp breath. *This is it*, she thought.

He continued. "When I was first going away, she declared her feelings for me, Rose. I must be completely honest with you."

"You need not tell," Rose said. "We can be friends, whatever. I know how things were."

"You do?"

"Yes, she told me at the time. You loved her. Perhaps you still do, and she is free again now, and if you give her a short space…"

"Rose, stop there," Michael interrupted her. He stood still and turned to her. "I had to tell her back then, I could not reciprocate her feelings. Too much was going on. And now, well, I need calm and tranquillity, Rose, not excitement and more living on the edge."

"But I always thought…" Rose stopped speaking.

Michael's words went around and around in her head, all the way home. Rose was sure that Delphi had told her Michael had returned Delphi's feelings.

Why had she said that? Was she envious of me? Surely not.

She arrived back home, her mind in turmoil.

I'm so angry right now I might say something I shall regret for a lifetime. She was young, we all were. But she was so hurtful on purpose. She must *have known exactly what she was doing.*

By the time she'd changed into her day dress, she was still seething.

Rose found Delphi in the garden, pretending to read. She sat with her shoulders hunched and a shawl around her. She didn't hold her head high in a show of artificial arrogance designed to fool the world into believing she cared nought for anything these days.

As Rose marched forwards, the springy grass silenced her footsteps. She glimpsed Delphi surreptitiously dabbing her eyes with a small white handkerchief and then the book fell to the ground. Rose's heart was hard. She had trained herself over the years to be restrained, to turn the other cheek, to be understanding and supportive. Well, no longer! She had earned this determination with a very long apprenticeship in self-effacement. At last she was going to stand her ground. Enough was enough.

"Delphi, how dare you? How could you have been so cruel and calculating?" she shouted at her sister.

Delphi stared at her with her handkerchief poised halfway to her eyes. Her face was a mask of surprise.

"You deceived me all those years ago. You deliberately tricked me into believing that Michael had told you he loved you when you wantonly flung yourself at him."

After a moment of silence, Delphi spoke. "I tried to tell you the other day. Rose, I'm sorry. I'm really sorry."

"But why? Why were you so deliberately cruel?"

"I was young; I was jealous of you."

"Jealous of me? Oh come on, really!"

"I was. You were at university. Everything was about you. Izzy was the baby darling and you were the focus of all the conversation."

"You had the same opportunities. You were too intent on play-acting and … and flirting your way around the area." Rose was still fuming and that added cruelty to her words. "You altered the course of my whole life."

"That's hardly fair. Michael wasn't ready for any romance, never mind with me."

Rose turned away, her eyes stinging. Then she sighed and, in that moment, she knew she had said enough, but her temper would smoulder for a long while. She had vented it for the time being, but this was not the end. She faced her sister again.

"Rose, I'm really truly sorry. I've changed. I've grown up a lot and my life is very, very different now."

The seed of the idea concerning Delphi's current state, formed in Rose's mind just a very few short weeks ago, took shape and started to grow. It would put Delphi out of harm's way with the gossips, and if Rose was honest with herself, it would place her sister out of her own way too for just long enough.

The idea would have to wait for the right moment. First Rose and Delphi must speak with their parents with the news of Delphi's impending confinement. It could not be hidden for much longer. Her waist was thickening, and even her face looked more rounded. Nor would it be long before Mr and Mrs Dight arrived.

CHAPTER 32

Rose soon had to confront the prospect of Michael's departure. Their time together had been so fleeting, and Rose was left in a welter of uncertainty. He had called her 'astonishing'. He had told her he did not have yearnings for her sister. After so many years of believing that to be so, she was having difficulty adjusting.

It doesn't mean he would take me, though, she thought, *despite what he said about needing my grace to help re-find his own.*

She met him outside the station on that dour day. It was a sunless, sombre place. The concourse was crowded with khaki-clad figures. A few, younger men in the main, had an air of animation and a lightning charge around them. Most were listless and sat propped against walls or leaned on their bags. A few civilians, mainly women dressed in joyless colours, stood next to some of the men — not touching, of course. Etiquette must prevail.

"Rose, you look lovely in that peach-coloured dress. It is much better to have this image of you when I leave rather than a melancholy one," said Michael.

She glanced up at him but felt her mouth wobble, so looked away quickly and noticed another young lady dab the corner of her eye surreptitiously. She had no gloves and Rose could see her wedding band. It seemed shiny and new.

"Everyone here must have the same hopes and fears," Rose said. "No one speaks of them, though. Each endures their own."

"It has to be that way to make it bearable."

"Yes." Conversation between them had become stilted and unnatural.

"Write to me soon, Rose. I need those little snippets of home and your tranquillity," Michael said in a conspiratorial voice, bending his head closer to her ear.

Then they turned and headed through the khaki whirlpool and through the barrier. Rose hurried past the engine with its plume of coal smoke and the glow from the firebox in the cab. All too soon Michael found his compartment on the train. The door slammed and the thread between them was cut with the clatter.

He appeared at a window not far away and Rose moved towards him, but she sensed his withdrawal. He was back in that other world; one she could not share, no matter how he spoke of his experiences and she tried to imagine it.

Through the grimy glass he watched her slight, girlish figure advancing parallel with the moving carriage. She quickened her stride until she could no longer keep up. She waved. He sensed her smile was brave. His heart lurched.

Am I waiting too long to declare what I'm thinking?

He desperately wanted to return and run from the station with Rose's hand in his, into the country hills, never to come back.

No! That's impossible. I have my duty to perform.

Looking at the soldier in the seat opposite, he saw a tunic stretched to tearing point over a large stomach. The man's moustache was over-long, and Michael had a disgusting image of him straining his soup through it. The codger belched slightly. Michael turned his head away, but the image remained.

This is what I am returning to. God! Peace must come eventually, surely. Concentrate on that thought alone.

"We can wait no longer, Delphi," Rose said with hardness in her voice.

"Oh, but I cannot, honestly. I am dreading it. You have no idea."

"All the more reason to get it said. Come along. Papa is in his study. If we go to him now it will be out, and then we may plan for the future."

Delphi remained in her chair with her head down and a damp rag of a handkerchief twisted between her fingers.

"Delphi. Now. Come." Rose was insistent. Her sister looked at her pleadingly. "This won't go away, so let us go and speak with Papa. He is not an ogre. He may not understand but he will be pragmatic, and we shall come up with a solution. I shall ask to talk to him about that. I have an idea."

Delphi prised herself from her seat and, with heavy legs and shoulders, turned to the door.

Rose sighed, for she was not without sympathy. "Come on, dearest."

They descended the stairs side by side and Rose crossed the hall to knock on the study door.

"One moment, I'm coming," Mr Strong said.

"Papa, Delphi and I have something important to discuss. We are sorry to disturb you, but this cannot wait."

The door opened.

"Come in, my children. What a pleasure." Then Mr Strong glimpsed Delphi's eyes before she cast them down, and his brow puckered.

Delphi sat in the chair opposite her father's and Rose stood beside her. Nobody spoke.

"Well? Speak up. I shall not bite," Mr Strong chuckled.

"Delphi has something to tell you and it may come as a surprise, but I feel sure you will understand," Rose said.

With some of her old spirit, Delphi took a deep breath and looked directly at her father. "Papa," she said, "I am to have George Dight's child. There, I've said it."

Mr Strong sat back in his chair, the smile disappeared, and he folded his arms. "I see."

There was silence. He stared at his middle daughter until Delphi lowered her eyes. The quiet was far more unnerving than a barrage of shouting.

Rose nipped her bottom lip. She awaited the torrent with apprehension. Her father was tolerant, but she knew some things would not be allowed, even though he liked to think of himself as a modernist. It was his household and his rules were to be followed.

He stood. He walked around behind his chair. Straightening his cuffs and smoothing his jacket he straightened his back, returning to sit once more. "Oh Delphi," he sighed. "Why do you always seem to cause us problems?"

As he shook his head, her tears started to fall. Rose knew his calm disappointment was harder to bear than almost anything, for although Delphi had seemed a rebellious child, they all respected their father greatly. Delphi craved his approval.

"Leave me now. I must decide what to say to your mother and come up with something that will prevent total disgrace for us all."

"Papa, may I have a word after Delphi has left?"

He nodded. "But please be brief."

"Yes, Papa."

As the door closed behind Delphi, Rose took her place in the chair opposite her father as he indicated.

"Perhaps there is a solution. I have not discussed this with anyone, not even Delphi, and it is just a fledgling notion."

"Oh Rose, the Dights are about to join us here for a while. We must keep this from them, whatever else. The shame is intolerable."

"Papa, I do believe George and Delphi would have wed if he had lived. This child will be the Dights' grandchild. They might help. What if she went to stay with them until after the child is born? It cannot be denied that no one locally would hear of it. After all, they do live some distance away."

"We know nothing of them, Rose. They live on the other side of the world!"

"She would return with the baby, of course, Papa. We could say her husband died abroad, which would be true. Why do we not keep this in mind when we meet them and decide after? Mrs Dight sounded so approachable and friendly in her letter to me."

"A letter is hardly enough upon which to make such a huge decision regarding your sister's future. We might be condemning her to any horror. I don't think this is an answer, Rose."

"Let us keep an open mind, at least. We are in a precarious position," Rose said.

"I do not need to be reminded of that, my child."

"No, Papa. Of course not. I apologise."

"When are the Dights due to arrive here? Remind me."

"At the end of next week, I understand."

"We shall meet them and get to know them a little while they are here. Say no more of this, Rose. I shall judge the moment and discuss the situation with your mother."

As she entered the hall, Rose noticed a letter from Michael. She recognised the writing on the envelope instantly. Each letter that arrived brought intense relief that he was still alive.

So much of life is fragile now, she thought. She opened the envelope and began reading straight away.

My very dear Rose,

Rose clutched the letter to her heart for a minute and then she reread his introduction. *Do I dare believe this? Am I truly that dear to him?* She read on:

Of course I cannot say where I am, but you will know I am in France again. The journey was not too bad, and I find I am fitting in here as if I had not been away. I miss my good friend George most sorely, though.

You may remember I told you briefly of an incident when we raided and took a German trench system back in the summer. The boy who remained ran for it with his arms raised. Do you recall, my dear? I have had to take some despicable actions, Rose. Things with which I need to come to terms if I am to survive. Perhaps that time when the young lad escaped with his life was part of my redemption for something that happened this week. It will always remind me that there must be a Guardian Angel for each of us.

I became separated from my unit. Making my way back, I fell asleep. It was only for a moment. Foolish, but I was exhausted. I had not slept for nearly two days. I awoke with a German touching my shoulder. I truly thought I'd had it. He seemed to be on his own, but he had a weapon and was in uniform. He guided me to the road. Can you believe that? He gesticulated and kept saying the word 'lastwagen' and 'Fahrzeuge'. He was telling me a lorry patrol was passing that way soon. I don't know how he knew or why he did this. I scrambled from the roadside ditch and hailed the first vehicle. When I turned to thank him, he was gone. He had disappeared into the woods behind. Why would he do that? Of course, it was not the same boy who had made a run from that trench, but maybe it was some kind of recompense. I do not understand it at all. This war makes no sense. It requires us to do evil and then something good happens.

That morning I watched the sun rise with new eyes, my dear, and thought of you. The night dew was clinging to the grass and sparkling. The sky gradually turned from pink to pale yellow and then soft blue. To me it was all the colours of your serenity. The sun looked huge and orange as it rose above the horizon. There were wreaths of mist in the valley and a lark arose and sang with joy for the day. I was so relieved to be alive and I felt new hope that we would meet again.

Dear Rose, bless you for your constancy and courage. I rubbed the little wooden head of your Fumsup once I was in that lorry. I am sure we will both return to you.

From Michael

Rose sat at the bottom of the stairs and reread the whole letter. She had elation in her heart that Michael was alive and that he had praised her so. Then she stood, turned and ran up to her room with a light tread.

CHAPTER 33

The Dights arrived by motor taxi wrapped up in thick coats and scarves against the autumn chill.

"Welcome to our home," Mrs Strong greeted them with her husband.

After everyone had their outdoor garments taken, Mrs Strong drew Mrs Dight towards the drawing room and the two men followed. The three sisters exchanged glances and brought up the rear. After some organising, the company was seated. A fire crackled in a friendly, comforting way and the rippling flames cast a warming glow around the company. Afternoon tea arrived and the formality of small talk commenced.

"I had not realised that you were a minister of the church, Mr Dight," Mr Strong began.

"I have a parish that covers many miles. Our town is small, but there are outlying farms and homes a long distance away. We have by need to be a relaxed community. More so than in England, I think."

It took a while to give everyone a cup of tea and refreshments. This custom eased the passage from ritual and protocol to more uninhibited conversation. After a while they each began to relax as they found some common ground.

However, the subject of George Dight was studiously avoided for the time being. No one was quite sure how to approach it. Eventually, Mr Strong broke the ice.

"Your son came here on leave with Mr Redfern, his colleague who lives locally. He was a charming man, I understand, and we are all sorry for his passing. He was a credit to you, his church and his country."

"Thank you. War is an enigma, and no one from any side is immune."

"Delphi, dear, come and sit beside me," Mrs Dight said, patting the empty seat. "We must be friends. George clearly was very fond of you and so will I be."

"You are very kind," Delphi replied, unsure what else to say.

"The saddest thing for us is that we have no one to carry on our name. Our daughter will, of course, take another and her children will not be Dights, and my husband has no brothers to carry the name."

Delphi glanced across at Rose, who gave the merest hint of a concerned smile.

Following their afternoon tea, the Dights retired to refresh themselves and rest before the evening meal.

"What do you think of them, Delphi?" Izzy enquired.

"They seem very kind and pleasant people," she responded. "They were likely to be, to have a son like George."

"You seemed to be deep in conversation for quite a while from what I could see. I couldn't really hear, though, from across the room."

"Oh Izzy, she was telling me of their life and a bit about George as a little boy. He used to climb a particular tree and sit among the branches for hours reading, apparently. If he wasn't doing that, he was riding a horse at breakneck speed through the countryside. He could go for miles without seeing a soul. We have no idea of the vastness of the country there."

"I cannot imagine travelling that far away," Izzy said.

"You are a little homebird. I think it would be a grand adventure to explore somewhere so different."

"We should all miss you if you went." Izzy gave her sister a hug.

"I've been away for several months already, Izzy."

"I know, and I hope you won't go back in a hurry."

Again, Delphi and Rose exchanged glances. Rose observed the trapped look on Delphi's countenance and came to her rescue.

"Delphi may have to go away again soon. It is her duty. But she will return, you lovely little noddle," she said with affection.

That evening dinner was a formal affair with all the Strongs' best silver and glassware on show. Dora had on her finest black dress and her apron was pristinely white and edged with lace. The ladies in their finery each looked their best. Their colours were subdued in respect for the loss of one so dear. The atmosphere was serious. Half the company could not help but remember why their paths had crossed and the others respected this and sympathised with their melancholy.

Again, Delphi sat with Mrs Dight and they chatted easily.

"To be honest, it is a relief to be able to talk with you," she said to the older matron, more relaxed. "You, of all people, understand my mood." She spoke quietly rather than for the whole company. Rose, sitting opposite, heard her words of unfeigned feeling.

By the end of the week the departure of the guests was nearing. Delphi felt they had become friends, as did Mr and Mrs Strong. There had been plenty of opportunity to learn about each other, and Delphi had asked many questions concerning George's early years and the circumstances of their living.

"Shall we walk in the garden, my dear?" Mrs Dight asked Delphi, who acquiesced willingly.

They linked arms and strolled towards the little summer house at the end of the lavender beds.

"It has been such a pleasure and a relief to get to know you, Delphi. I understand why George thought so highly of you. Not only are you beautiful, but you are clever too. In other circumstances I can see that you would have opinions and be lively and interesting. It would have been a delight to welcome you into our family as my son's wife."

"Mrs Dight, I have something to say that I think you have a right to know before you leave," Delphi said. "I have put off telling you this for reasons I know you will understand, but I have no idea how you will accept this information. I adored your son and he loved me. Of that I am sure."

"Absolutely, my dear. I am certain of this too."

"I've dreaded this moment but as I said, you have a right to know." Delphi sat in silence.

"Tell me, my dear child. Nothing can be that bad or cannot be sorted."

CHAPTER 34

"Rose, I should welcome your company for this. I have put off sharing Delphi's condition with your mother. It might have been better to say before, but I was considering your suggestion after all. I needed to meet Mr and Mrs Dight."

When Mr Strong told his wife, she sank down upon the nearest chair and he had to send for smelling salts.

"Here you are, sir," Dora said. "Let me see to her. She'll be right as rain, you'll see. Don't fret, now."

And of course she was, but not until she had wept and shared her grief and worry with her husband.

"What are we to do? We shall be ruined. No one will want to speak to me and the girls' chances, never mind Delphi's, will be in tatters. How could she be so wanton, so lacking in thought for herself and others? And we have the Dights here. Surely they will be shocked to be staying in such a house as ours."

"Hush, my dear. You'll make yourself ill again. We shall work through this."

"She has always been a difficult child; she constantly questions authority, forever wanting *her* own way. What did I do to deserve this? What did I do wrong? What do we do about George's parents? They must not know of our shame. Hector died serving his country and Delphi does this to us. How could she?" She stood and started pacing about the room. "They need not hear anything. They will be going soon. Delphi can go and stay with my great aunt in Scarborough, perhaps. You must think of a story. We must outlive this crisis."

"I asked Rose to join us. She has an idea. I didn't share this news with you sooner because I wanted to consider the idea and meet the Dights. They could be involved."

Mrs Strong looked at her husband with raised eyebrows.

Delphi had spent long hours thinking through her moves and motivation before acting. She thought of Mrs Dight's words about not having a child to carry on the family name. It would be easier to run away and hide, but she owed this information to George's mother. She was a good person, and so was her husband.

"Let us sit for a moment," Delphi said, indicating the little covered seat at the end of the lavender walk. "It is sheltered from the breeze and the scent of the flowers is calming." She turned to face her companion and composed herself. "You may be shocked by this, but I hope you will understand. Your son … George and I … George expected that we might marry, and I would have dearly loved that. We got as far as submitting the papers to the ministry. Circumstances dictated otherwise." She paused. "The last time we were together was a beautiful day. It was a day from heaven." Delphi sat silently for a moment. "Mrs Dight, I … I'm expecting George's child." She shivered as a cool breeze stole into their retreat.

"Oh!" The matron took a deep breath. "I see."

"We loved each other deeply. He was in my soul and I in his." Delphi's eyes smarted and tears formed. "I know it was wrong, but over in France circumstances were so different, so dire and frightening. George was terrified, which made his going back to the front all the more brave. I just desperately needed to give him some comfort and something to remember, something to live for, I thought. I wanted him to stay with me forever. I'm so sorry. I understand if you are horrified."

"Not horrified. No, not that. Shocked, maybe, but the thought of my dear boy being terrified is hopelessly, unimaginably terrible to a mother. You must have helped him come to terms with his return."

They sat together for several moments and let the full import of Delphi's confession sink in.

Eventually, Mrs Dight spoke. "What will you do? I know little of English society, but I am sure things might be very difficult for you here and for your family."

"I don't know. Go away somewhere far from here, I suppose; at least until after our child is born. I don't want him, or her, to suffer any stigma. I don't wish to sully George's memory in any way. This baby is his too, and I shall endeavour to ensure he knows his father was a brave, brave soldier and a good man. Truly I should like to give the child George's surname. Would that offend you?"

"I wish we could help. As you say, this is our son's child too. No, I should not be affronted by that. Not at all. We Australians are more liberal and broad-minded than many English, I think."

They sat quietly together for several minutes. Mrs Dight stared into the future and Delphi remembered her past and the short time that she and George had had together. At least she had a permanent part of him now.

November 1916
Dearest Rose,

This cold is grinding us all down. It is the worst thing. Worse even than the shelling because it is relentless. I came close to tears; I am ashamed to tell you. We have been ordered not to remove our boots but the temptation in the dug-out is almost beyond endurance. I have my sheepskin jacket wrapped around my feet as I write but I am shivering, and the writing is wobbly as you see.

You know that the battles of the Somme are about done and whilst I cannot tell you where we are headed, it is no secret that it will be east.

My dearest, please send me some socks if you are able. I am in dire need.

The trenches here are thick with ice, but sometimes it is thin and if we break through then the water is so cold. There are wooden duckboards for us to walk along but they are narrow. Yesterday we were behind a fellow who was carrying two buckets of ammo as he headed towards the front line. They were heavy and he put them down to rest. Well, no one could get by, but the poor chap was exhausted. Someone tried to go around him and fell off the duckboards into the water, which came halfway up to his knees. That poor chap will regret his impatience for a long time. He will be lucky if he doesn't lose his toes at the very least.

Sorry, my dear. That is not what I should be writing. I am being insensitive to your sensibilities, but life is just so, so difficult at the moment.

I remember you said in your last letter that George's parents were going to visit your family. If I have not lost the opportunity, please tell them he was the best and bravest companion any chap could have and that he is sorely missed. I shall treasure memories of him all my life.

I have those to carry me forwards, thank the Lord. Your sweet smile and sunny nature are my blessings too, and my salvation. Please write to me soon, dearest Rose.

Your steadfast friend,

Michael

P.S. I hope Thom is not resentful of our friendship. I know he and you are close, but your letters do help me to cope with this hell hole.

Rose took her letter and went in search of Mrs Dight to share Michael's words referring to her son. Not finding her indoors, she donned her outdoor clothing and opened the door into the garden. She found George's mother returning along the lavender walk with Delphi. Their arms were linked.

Before Rose could read Michael's praise, Delphi spoke. "I have shared my condition with Mrs Dight, Rose."

Rose glanced across at the lady and tried to gauge her reaction, but it was impossible.

"This must be very difficult for you," Rose said to her. She could think of little else.

"I wish we did not live so far away. I should like to play a part in the life of George's child," Mrs Dight said.

"I, too, would have liked that," Delphi replied with sincerity.

"I must speak with my husband, now. Please forgive and excuse me." She unhooked Delphi's arm and departed.

Rose and Delphi watched her go.

"Maybe I should have said nothing, but I felt she had a right to know," Delphi said. "She so wants their name to continue."

"She seems to look at circumstances in a very different way to that which our neighbours here might," Rose said. "Delphi, have you thought about where you might go for your confinement?"

"Not really, but I should like to get right away. I want to start a new life, Rose, free of the stifling guilt I feel and the pain I see in Mama's eyes when she looks at me. I didn't receive that from George's mother. These Australians seem to view things in a much more modern way. I want my child to be free from blame, too."

CHAPTER 35

December 1916

Dear Rose,

I cannot wait longer to send you this because I need you to understand how I feel. I was determined to delay until this conflict is ended, but then I thought of George and you might never know what is in my mind.

My very dear Rose, this war has taught me that I crave calm and tranquillity, not just now while I am involved in such cruel and savage times, but for the peace of my soul when this is over.

Rose, I can picture your beautiful grey eyes as I write. I see in my mind's eye your soft hair. I sense your graceful spirit. If I survive this conflict, I would like to ask you to be my wife; to share with me my life and to go forward together in peace and love to build our own family. In short, I love you, Rose. I think I have for a very long time, but I closed my heart to it because I was confused by the difference between loyalty and duty to this country that I serve. I am no longer in such chaos of feelings. I know where my love and loyalty lie first and as soon as I can finish my duty, I shall return to you.

I hope this does not come as a shock to you, Rose, and that you had some idea of how my affections have grown into love. We have all changed over these past few years. If you have stronger feelings or an understanding with Thom, then I apologise and please forget this.

Please write to me as soon as you have considered my words. I really need to know your thoughts. If you accept my interest, I should like to approach your father upon my return.

With fondest best wishes,

Michael

Rose reread every word twice and then she cried. She wept for squandered lives and wasted time.

She crossed the floor to her wooden chest and pulled out her box of treasures. In it were all the letters Michael had ever sent to her. The little handkerchief with the rose in the corner was also there, and she thought back to that day when fighting with sticks was a portent of what was to come. She raised the small square of cloth to her cheek as she had done many times before. Its softness kissed her skin and she smiled at last.

"Delphi, my dear," Mrs Dight said as she skimmed down the stairs.

Despite her middle years, she was slim and lithe. The pale grey feathers that trimmed her dress floated around the neckline, complementing the sober dark hue of the fabric and adding vibrancy to her approach.

Delphi looked up and gave a wan smile. The sky was a heavy shade of slate and no rays of sun penetrated to liven up either her mood or the ground outside, which was still soggy from the night's downpour. She felt like an interloper in her own home. Her mother had barely spoken to her after an initial outburst following the news of Delphi's disgrace. Her father stood in the middle, trying to maintain an uneasy armistice.

"May I speak with you?" Mrs Dight had a pleading look in her eyes.

"Shall we go into the drawing room? Mama is in her bedroom and the girls are busy upstairs too."

Mrs Dight sat on the sofa and reached for Delphi's hand. She seemed ill at ease suddenly, and the animation of moments before dissipated. "I've spoken with Mr Dight, my dear. I've also spoken with your father and mother about your situation.

I believe your Mama is joining us directly. I understand your family's point of view. It is difficult for them."

At that moment, Mrs Strong entered the room. George's mother stood and indicated the place next to Delphi, but Mrs Strong sat to one side of the fireplace.

"Our visitors have been extremely kind to you, Delphi," Mrs Strong said. "They are offering a way forward, for which you can be very grateful indeed."

Delphi glanced at her companion, who was smiling benignly, and then at her mother, who was not. She looked at Mrs Strong with some of her old provocation, but in truth she felt frightened. All she needed was a comforting arm.

"May I?" Mrs Dight raised querying eyebrows across the room and received a response that indicated she should proceed. "Mr Dight and I wondered if you might return with us to Australia for your confinement. It is a long way from your home, I know, but we would treasure your company and that of your little one when your time comes. Of course, you would come home when you wish, but it might help your family out of a tight spot, Delphi." She squeezed Delphi's hand and smiled warmly. It was the comfort that she craved at that moment and tears fell.

"It's too late for tears, Delphi. You have brought shame on our family," her mother said. "I think it is a very kind offer indeed, considering the effect you could have on all our lives with your recent behaviour. There is the possibility of going to stay with Great Aunt Beatrice in Scarborough, but even there you might be known."

There was silence for a moment. Delphi raised shining eyes to George's mother and nodded. "Thank you. Thank you so much. I will not let you down. I owe George the world, and I wish to repay him and his family with my loyalty. What I would love most of all is that his baby might carry his name into the future."

"My dear child." Mrs Dight managed to control her tears before they fell.

A whirl of activity ensued over the next two days. There were clothes to be organised, packing to do, and an extra ticket to be sought. That proved tricky, but Mr Strong called upon his employer to lend his voice to the persuasion. The telephone at his place of work was such a necessity these days and came in handy now. In the end a reservation was made, and arrangements were completed for the collection of the ticket at Plymouth from where the return voyage was to leave.

On the morning of departure, Rose called Delphi to her room.

"I have finished this for you." Rose held out a small painting in the palm of her hand. "I hope it does justice but if you are not satisfied with it, I should understand."

"Oh, Rose." Delphi's eyelashes glistened as she looked carefully at the image. "It is so vividly authentic. His eyes follow me. They have that spark that he had in life. I feel I could slide my fingers through his hair."

There were many tears shed that morning. Despite her previous words, Mrs Strong clung to her wayward daughter while Izzy and Rose held each other and wept. Promises were made to write as soon as possible with entreaties to describe all in detail.

Mr Strong decided to accompany the Dights and Delphi as far as Manchester and see them safely aboard the train to London, where they would change for the one to take them into the West Country and their ship.

"Delphi, if there is anything, anything at all, about which you wish to tell me after you have landed, please write forthwith. Australia is such a long way, but I shall ensure you have a passage home anytime you want to return."

"Papa, this is an adventure of a lifetime. It is an opportunity not to be wasted, but thank you for that."

"I hope we will meet again before too much time has passed," Mr Strong said, but they both knew that was unlikely.

CHAPTER 36

Having received Michael's letter, Rose was impatient to speak with her father. It was impossible with all that was happening with Delphi. Yet again her sister was causing havoc in the household and everyone was running rings around her. Rose caught her resentment and squashed it as best she could.

I'm becoming more like her as she becomes like me, she thought. *I was always the calm one who knew my mind. Now I'm sounding belligerent while she is thinking things through.*

"Papa," she said the day after Delphi's departure. Her father's study door was ajar, and he turned at her knock. "I have a letter, part of which I wish to share with you. It's from Michael."

"Come in, Rose, my child."

"Papa, these are strange times in which we live, and things are changing by the month. Society's traditions are altering in so many ways. Please, I would like to read part of this to you."

Rose took her time in finding the appropriate passages. She had her own confusions with which to contend. She felt awkward in sharing some of Michael's thoughts, but he was eloquent in the expression of his love.

"I still need your permission, Papa, but I would like to have your blessing to respond positively to him. I know I'm twenty-one now, but he will still come to speak with you. That's impossible at the moment, of course," she said.

"He has always been a deep thinker. I remember when you were little more than children still and he visited here. He spoke with intelligence of the political events of that time. He has prospects too. His father runs a very respectable business in this town." Mr Strong sat in his large leather chair with his elbows resting on the arms. He steepled his fingers as he thought aloud. He sat forwards and idly shifted the papers on the table next to him.

"I don't think he wants to go into his father's business, though," Rose said. "He was at teacher training college when war broke out."

"True, very true. I suppose we shall see."

Rose was becoming impatient with the reminiscing and ruminating. She wanted an answer from her father, but she would not presume to rush him. Then she could resist no longer. "Papa, I shan't need your permission, but I would like your blessing," Rose repeated.

"All my children leaving me. Hector, Delphi and now you," he said.

"Well, not yet. I would like to be able write to him with my answer, though."

"Do you want to marry him, Rose? It's a big step. He may be much changed by this war."

"Yes, Papa, I do. We have corresponded regularly and when he was home on leave, we spent time together. We share many interests."

"Very well, write and tell him your answer, and while I should like to see him, you are right. You no longer need my permission. I see you are bolder, Rose. You have grown up a lot."

Rose came up behind his chair, put her arms around him and kissed his cheek, feeling the prickles beneath her lips and smelling his musky cologne that was so familiar.

It was so strange to have a long-distance courtship. Rose's letters to Michael were full of love, now that she could utter it freely, as well as detailed descriptions of the fields and paths around their home and little events of her daily life.

Mr Lloyd George succeeded Mr Asquith as Prime Minister, Christmas came and went and that winter of 1916-17 was the worst on record, with the cold being unbearable at times. Michael still managed to express small signs of positivity and his letters were full of love for Rose and of hope.

The newspapers spoke of the troubles in Russia, and information seeping from France and Belgium was depressing in the extreme, where conditions for troops were appalling with massive losses on both sides. The United States of America severed relations with Germany at the beginning of February 1917. Things were hotting up yet again around Ypres because of its strategic importance in controlling all the routes to the mineral-rich lands around. There were rumours of a forthcoming battle to gain the ground involving the Messines Ridge to the south of that town.

It was around then that Rose lost touch with Michael.

CHAPTER 37

July 1917

Michael lay listening as he had done many times before. This time, though, he was surrounded by the stench of rotting meat, coming from his dead compatriots. He closed his eyes and tried not to breathe through his nostrils.

The battle had been an endless grind of attrition, with allies and enemy losing hundreds of men daily. Surely this was the most costly effort yet. Even the blood of the Somme did not match this. Ypres was such a strategic treasure. Allies' ownership was critical to destroying German submarine bases on the Belgian coast. Both sides were throwing all they had to keep or gain it. The long ridge started in the north and was known as Passchendaele, after the village there. It ran all the way around the east and down to Messines in the south. It was key to the main objective because the Germans held it and could rain down armaments upon the Allies in and around the town.

"At least the bombardment is over," Michael whispered to his companion.

"Yeah, ten bloody days and nights."

"It's peppered the ground with holes and this rain's going to make it very hard going. It's like treacle out here. The shells have damaged the drainage system. See that pipe sticking up? We need to get back now and report all this."

"Righty-o, sir."

"The breeze is coming down off the ridge too. Just right for a gas attack. Don't want to be caught out here."

"Blimey, no, sir. Let's get the hell out of it, then."

They slithered through the mud, keeping low.

"The land is so … flat here, and I gather … this is the worst rain in … thirty years," Michael puffed. The effort of moving through the swamp was tremendous.

"Gas, gas, gas!" The cry went up along the line as Michael and his companion slid into the trench system. The sound of gongs added to the mêlée. Everyone was putting on masks and fingers fumbled in their haste. Pandemonium appeared to reign as men turned from dugouts with bayonets fixed to man the fire step. Others adjusted helmets and gas hoods and ran with buckets of ammo. An infantry attack could follow and frequently did.

"The taste of this rubber tube and the smell of the fabric is vile," a private shouted across the intervening space.

"Never mind that. Get it tucked in properly or you'll be sorry," Michael said.

"I know that. A company man at the last show didn't put his on quick enough. He dropped like a rock, clutching his throat. He had a few spasms and twists and that was that. He went west."

Somebody else added, "Yeah, we had a little dog, a scruffy mongrel thing. He died too. It was 'orrible to watch. He lay there with 'is two little paws over 'is nose. All covered in mud 'e was, and just lying there."

"Okay men, enough of that. Think about what you're doing, or you'll be next."

"That's the eighteen-pounders doing their best to disperse this lot," the corporal said as a loud crump shook the earth.

"Here they come!" The cry echoed along the trench.

Rifles and machine guns spat and rattled. In the fog of smoke and noise Michael saw a line of Germans, bayonets glistening, reach the wire.

"Their shells have destroyed it. Watch out!"

A crack and clink of gunfire ensured a pile of bodies fell or hung motionless on what was left of the defence. Others followed behind.

Then, Michael's skull seemed to burst from a roaring clack by his ear. His head began to swim, his throat became dry and his lungs felt heavy. He saw the trench winding like a snake and sandbags appeared to float all around. There was a rushing waterfall of noise. His knees buckled and he sank to the ground. All went black.

"I've had no letter for weeks. It is so unlike him not to write, and yet I've no bad news either. I am sick with worry. What should I do?" Rose spoke to her commanding officer in Manchester.

"There is little you can do, I'm afraid. You know as well as I do, Miss Strong, that the notices of deaths pass through these offices for our regiments. You deal with them on a daily basis. And there's as many simply disappearing as being notified to us. The French had a major disaster at the Nivelle offensive and then they had blasted mutineers. Because of all that, strategies of General Haig have been very costly. That's why he's throwing everything he can at the Hun. The attrition may be paying off, though. I'm sorry, Miss Strong, but you'll have to wait like everyone else."

"Sir," she said and crept out of his office.

That evening, around the family dinner table, her pallid face was noticed.

"What's the matter, Rose?" asked Izzy.

"I'm just a little worried," she answered. "I haven't heard from Michael for quite a while now."

"It doesn't necessarily mean bad news," her mother said. "Does it?"

"I really don't know, Mama, but it's not good."

"I am sure all will be well. Just have patience, Rose. Please let us change the subject. Dora has produced a delicious meal here. We owe her our enjoyment of it without depressing talk." Mrs Strong was increasingly reluctant to participate in talk of matters overseas. Since Hector's passing, she had little patience.

After dinner, Rose disappeared to her room to write yet another letter that would probably go unanswered. The lack of information was worse than bad news, she decided.

CHAPTER 38

Monday 16th July 1917

My dearest Rose,

I am writing to you from Étaples. Eatables, our boys call it. It's on the coast of France, so I am closer to you now. There is a vast hospital complex here. Do not fret, I am alive but currently I'm having a bit of trouble speaking. Well, I've lost my voice completely.

My gas helmet sprung a leak courtesy of a stray bullet during an attack. By good fortune, however, the mud in the bottom of the trench plugged the hole and I only got a small amount of it. It's the cause of my lack of voice, though, and I can give no orders without a voice.

The best news is that I am on my way home. Yes, I'm coming back to you, my dearest. I'm not sure exactly when, but it won't be long. There are about four miles of hospital tents here, but I think my bed will be needed by others, so they won't keep me longer than necessary. There's talk of me going to a sanatorium on the coast somewhere when I return. I think I am finished with this show. There're rumbles of a discharge on grounds of ill health. I've flirted with death and now I shall love my life with you by my side. My dear heart, I can hardly wait until we are together again.

This morning at sunrise I stood on the estuary of the river here and watched the fishing fleet leave. Rose, the water was like a mirror, so still was it. Each small boat with its brown sail was reflected in the surface. I almost believed the world was normal. It was so peaceful and beautiful. I cannot understand my luck in being here, alive.

Apparently in peacetime it used to be a favourite spot for artists. You would love the light quality, I understand. For a while this morning the sound of guns was stilled, and I heard birdsong again.

The doctor wants to have another look at me. I shall finish this later. XXX 'til then.

Tuesday 17th July

I have in my possession letters to bring with me when I leave here NEXT MONDAY! I shall come from Dover to London and then on to Manchester by train. I shall see you shortly, my love.

I must visit the hospital as soon as possible after my return so that they might investigate my throat. That's it for me in this show. I shall not have to return. If you can put up with a croaky old lag, life will be unbelievably good.

Perhaps you will be able to verify what time the train arrives and meet me. I should be getting into Manchester at about 5.30 in the afternoon on Wednesday 25th July, I am told. I have travel permits but will have to stay overnight in London.

Oh, my dearest Rose, I can hardly believe I shall see you so soon.

In the meantime, I send you my best love.

Michael

Rose ran through the house waving the envelope and shouting to anyone who might be around to hear.

"He's alive! Mama, Izzy, I have a letter from Michael. He's all right. Dora, do you hear? Michael is alive!"

Mrs Strong came from her bedroom to the top of the stairs and met her eldest daughter, who came running up, clutching her skirts to avoid a fall. Breathlessly Rose flung herself into her mother's arms.

"Rose, I am so pleased for you. Truly, I am so relieved," she said.

"What is it? What did you say?" Izzy rushed out. "What is all the commotion about?"

"I have a letter. Michael has been in hospital, but he is alive. He's coming home. NEXT WEEK!"

Izzy clapped her hands and hugged her sister with vehemence. "That is such happy news, Rose. What a relief."

Dora rolled into the hall, wiping her fingers on a cloth. Rose scampered down the stairs to greet her and waved the envelope. "Michael is coming home next week." She beamed her pleasure at the old family retainer.

"Oh, Miss Rose, that's very good news."

Rose could hardly contain her joy and excitement. She'd had several days to wait, and now here she was on the station platform awaiting the train bearing her love home to her. It had been such a long and tense time recently, but all those feelings had dissipated with the arrival of the letter at the end of last week.

She looked up at the massive station clock. Ten minutes.

She glanced up again. Five minutes.

Again, she could not resist looking. Two minutes.

She saw in the distance the puff of steam and the long dark shape took form as it edged closer and closer. She could see the outlines of the windows, the doors of the carriages. She felt the vibration as the great monster trundled and clanked its way past her and along the platform.

She turned to ask a passing porter, "Is this the train from London, please?"

"Yes, petal," he answered in his strong Mancunian accent.

She stood on her tiptoes to peer over the heads of all the people waiting on the platform. A great waft of steam arose with a loud hiss and she stepped back in agitation.

Doors banged.

People shouted.

Khaki mixed with colourful finery.

This was such a different scene from that when they said goodbye. The air was charged with anticipation and joy.

Gradually the crowds thinned, and Rose still did not see him. She moved forwards and wove through the remaining throng. Many were leaving. Where was he? She could not have missed him. She started to hurry along the length of the train. Her breath came in great gulps, hurting her throat.

She peered through grimy windows into each carriage. The guard blew a whistle and there was another loud hiss from the engine.

"Wait, please wait!" Was that her own voice?

Soon she would run out of platform. Surely, he could not have missed the train in London.

And then she saw him. His blond head leaned against the window and his eyes were closed. He was in a deep sleep.

Rose waved and flagged down a station worker. "Excuse me, my fiancé is still on board," she gasped at him. "He's been ill. He's returning from the front. He is sleeping, I think."

"All right, flower, leave it to me," he said.

Rose watched him run to the guard to explain. She wanted to tap on the window, but it might startle Michael and if he was unwell it would not help. His face was pallid and there were dark rings around his eyes. As she watched, the man in uniform boarded the train and made his way along to Michael's carriage.

"'Ere, matey," she heard through the open window. "Your girl's waiting for you, me old cock. Time to wake up." Though gruff, he spoke gently.

Rose paced. She couldn't keep still. Michael stirred and looked around. She saw the expression of surprise on his face, and then it was replaced by the biggest smile she had ever seen him give. He stood a little shakily and edged to the carriage door. The station employee thrust the door back and handed his bag down onto the platform.

Convention be hanged. Love like this made the world around her vanish. Any people were silenced, the hissing of the engine faded. The smell of the steam dispersed, and she took leave of her normal sensibilities. Here was her returning cavalier; her champion; her love. She flung herself towards him.

"Welcome home," she said.

The silence enveloped her. His enfolding arms became her world. She looked up at him and felt his lips on hers, warm and soft, becoming hard and passionate. She would remember this moment all her life.

With one arm encircling her, for he could not let her go, he dug deep into his pocket and pulled something from within. He opened his fist and there lying in the palm of his hand was her little good luck Fumsup.

A NOTE TO THE READER

Dear Reader,

Thank you so much for reading *Sisters at War*. This has been the first book in a series, which features relationships during turbulent times during the first half of the twentieth century. The inspiration for the character of Rose came from my granny, who did have two sisters and a brother. It's most definitely not her story, but she was a thoughtful and caring lady who always tried to see beyond the bad that people might do and appreciate the reasons. This was Rose, although in the book, she was too considerate of others and ultimately needed to stand up for herself and be less self-effacing.

When I lived in northern France I spent many hours visiting battle sites on the Somme and at Ypres in Belgium where there are fascinating museums, as well as at Vimy Ridge, Arras and Newfoundland Park where I was privileged to lay a wreath on behalf of the Royal British Legion. My husband and I were even invited to a reburial of soldiers discovered during building works, which was particularly interesting as we spoke at length to the person charged with using DNA to trace relatives of those long missing. Ceremonies at the Thiepval monument and the Lochnagar mine crater give an idea of the scale of destruction during those war years that survive to this day. This led to visits to the National Archives at Kew to research my grandfather's World War One experiences and I discovered his name in the war diaries written at the time, all of which provided inspiration for this story.

We discovered my grandfather was a scout during the war and frequently had to go into no man's land and lie listening for many hours. As he was attached to his battalion headquarters, he is named in the war diaries written in the trenches at the time. With this information, we were able to go and walk, almost in his footsteps, one hundred years later and see the woodland which has regrown, the slopes he must have crossed and the villages he was involved in securing.

The city of Ypres was rebuilt in the image of the previous place, so all the building are as they were, despite being almost flattened during the period of constant battles. Its's a beautiful city and well worth a visit. The daily ceremony at the Menin Gate, when the local fire brigade honour the dead, by playing the last post, is both eerie and emotional as the bugles echo around the massive stonework covered in names of the fallen.

I first discovered a Fumsup, sometimes called a Touchwud, when I was given one after my grandfather died. Although they were designed at the beginning of the twentieth century, they became particularly popular during World War One when they were given to soldiers as good luck mementoes. I have a collection of nearly forty now and they are all slightly different. Some are rare, while others reflect the multicultural aspect of the war. One I have, holds a kukri knife while another sits cross-legged and has a tiny nutshell for a turban. Most are as described in the book, often with coloured eyes to reflect the birth month of the recipient or with tiny black and white beads for eyes.

I do hope, if you enjoyed *Sisters at War*, you might consider writing a short review on Amazon or Goodreads. These, from knowledgeable people, are so important for authors' success but also contribute to other readers' choice of a book.

If you would like to know more about my writing, my website is www.rosrendleauthor.co.uk. You can also sign up for my newsletter via my website. I often give free gifts and there is early access and information about my books. I love to hear from readers, and you are able to connect with me through Facebook or via Twitter. I hope we'll meet again in the pages of my other novels.

Ros Rendle

Sapere Books is an exciting new publisher of brilliant fiction and popular history.

To find out more about our latest releases and our monthly bargain books visit our website:
saperebooks.com